Who would sh

A week ago the very question would've been unthinkable. Brognola's friendship with the Executioner had been cemented long before she came on board—before there was a team to join, in fact. If anyone had asked her, Barbara Price would have said it was impossible for anyone to break that bond of trust.

And she would have been wrong.

Disgusted with herself, she lifted the receiver and tapped the big Fed's office number. It rang three times, and Price decided she would give up after four, her duty done, when Brognola picked up.

"Brognola." Was the man as weary as he sounded, or was she projecting her own emotional fatigue?

"It's me," she said, and closed her eyes. "We got a call."

MACK BOLAN ®
The Executioner

DON PENDLETON'S

THE EXECUTIONER®

SHIFTING SHADOWS

The Conspiracy Trilogy

BOOK II

A GOLD EAGLE BOOK FROM
WORLDWIDE®

TORONTO • NEW YORK • LONDON
AMSTERDAM • PARIS • SYDNEY • HAMBURG
STOCKHOLM • ATHENS • TOKYO • MILAN
MADRID • WARSAW • BUDAPEST • AUCKLAND

For Rosemary Nelson, human-rights attorney,
assassinated by Protestant guerrillas in Lurgan,
County Armagh, Northern Ireland, on March 15, 1999.
God keep.

The fight goes on.

First edition April 2001
ISBN 0-373-64269-5

Special thanks and acknowledgment to
Michael Newton for his contribution to this work.

SHIFTING SHADOWS

It is fatal to enter any war without the will to win it.
—General Douglas MacArthur

War is cruelty, and you cannot refine it.
—General William T. Sherman

Our enemies are more accustomed to inflicting damage
than receiving it. They're used to people cowering in
fear. I plan to change that, here and now.
—Mack Bolan

THE
MACK BOLAN®

LEGEND

Nothing less than a war could have fashioned the destiny of the man called Mack Bolan. Bolan earned the Executioner title in the jungle hell of Vietnam.

But this soldier also wore another name—Sergeant Mercy. He was so tagged because of the compassion he showed to wounded comrades-in-arms and Vietnamese civilians.

Mack Bolan's second tour of duty ended prematurely when he was given emergency leave to return home and bury his family, victims of the Mob. Then he declared a one-man war against the Mafia.

He confronted the Families head-on from coast to coast, and soon a hope of victory began to appear. But Bolan had broken society's every rule. That same society started gunning for this elusive warrior—to no avail.

So Bolan was offered amnesty to work within the system against terrorism. This time, as an employee of Uncle Sam, Bolan became Colonel John Phoenix. With a command center at Stony Man Farm in Virginia, he and his new allies—Able Team and Phoenix Force—waged relentless war on a new adversary: the KGB.

But when his one true love, April Rose, died at the hands of the Soviet terror machine, Bolan severed all ties with Establishment authority.

Now, after a lengthy lone-wolf struggle and much soul-searching, the Executioner has agreed to enter an "arm's-length" alliance with his government once more, reserving the right to pursue personal missions in his Everlasting War.

1

There are language police in Quebec. They don't wear uniforms or carry guns. Instead, they dress in casual attire, armed with clipboards and Polaroid cameras. Their mission, under law, is to insure that every place of business in the province recognizes French as the official language. Proprietors are free to advertise in English, but if they do so, they must also advertise in French, with French inscription being significantly larger than the English text.

Size matters, after all.

Mack Bolan was acquainted with Quebec. The last time he had visited the province he was hunting terrorists affiliated with the Quebec Liberation Front, who had allied themselves with members of the stateside Mafia to wreak bloody havoc around Montreal. That war was ancient history, but the man known as the Executioner had returned. This time around, the human predators he sought spoke Russian.

The action had begun in Arizona. Bolan's brother, Johnny Bolan Gray, was caught up in a missing-person case that swiftly turned into a life-or-death evasion exercise, involving the Russian Mafia. Bolan had helped his brother turn the game around, going on the offensive, but it was still an uphill fight. The Russian mobsters were apparently allied, to some unknown extent, with agents of the CIA, the goals and motives of the players still obscure. More troubling still was Hal Brognola, director of Sensitive Operations Group, adamantly refusing to involve himself, or the ultracovert Stony Man Farm, beyond the barest minimum of information gathering.

That reticence was troubling, granted. But far worse, to Bolan's mind was what might lie behind it, hidden like a viper poised to strike.

He was relieved to be in Montreal and on the brink of combat. It would help to take his mind off Washington and Stony Man. If he wasn't completely focused on the here and now, there was no reason to believe he would survive.

"This is Valerik's place?" Johnny asked.

"One of them."

"And you think he's here?"

"I've got my fingers crossed," Bolan replied.

Tolya Valerik was the Russian *mafioso* they had chased across country, from Los Angeles to New York City, narrowly missing the target each time. He had helicoptered out of their last trap on Long Island, leaving his soldiers to fight a losing rear-guard action, and two full days had been lost before the Executioner found an informant to squeeze, confirming Bolan's fear that Valerik had fled the U.S.

Still, it could've been worse. Europe, for instance, or even Russia. For reasons best known to himself, Valerik had fallen back on Montreal, staying closer to the action and his fairweather friends at Langley. This way, he could cross the border any time he wanted to, no one the wiser.

If he lived.

Parked across the street from an apartment house on Boulevard Labelle, Johnny at the wheel of their rented Mercury Cougar XR7, Bolan hoped they would be able to take the Russian alive. There were questions that needed to be answered, for his own peace of mind, quite possibly for national security.

But first, of course, they had to *find* Valerik.

The apartment house was one of three addresses his informant had provided, swearing on his life—or what was left of it—that Valerik used all three on visits to Quebec. The other two locations were a smaller flat on Mont-Royal, and what their pigeon called a "party house" in Boucherville, across the St. Lawrence. It came down to a mental coin toss in the end, and here they were, the dashboard clock reminding Bolan that it would be midnight in another thirteen minutes.

Time to move.

"Let's do it," Bolan said.

"Damn right," his brother echoed from the driver's seat.

They had been forced to travel light and pick up hardware on arrival from a contact in Laval. The brothers had packed their standard side arms in their check-through luggage for the red-eye flight to Montreal, a .40-caliber Glock 23 for Johnny, Bolan's selective-fire Beretta 93-R and the more powerful .44 Magnum Desert Eagle. The dealer in Laval had fixed them up with a matched set of MP-5 SD-3 submachine guns—the Heckler & Koch models with telescoping metal stocks and built-in sound suppressors—plus spare magazines, a stockpile of 9 mm Parabellum ammunition and a dozen M-26 fragmentation grenades.

With any luck, Bolan thought, it would be all the hardware they'd need. A tidy hit-and-git would suit him fine, after the bloody chaos in L.A. and New York, the mayhem yet to come, if his suspicions of CIA involvement with the Russian Mob should prove correct.

One easy job, he thought. That was all they needed. Just one.

And Bolan heard a cold voice in his head telling him not to hold his breath.

They left the car and locked it, caught a lull in traffic, crossing in the middle of the block. Both men were dressed in casual elegance, befitting their high-rent destination, but with open collars, side-arms and submachine guns concealed by their matching black trench coats. At a glance, they might have been accountants, lawyers, businessmen. It took a closer look, behind the eyes, to understand their deadly purpose, and you only saw it then if you already knew what you were looking for.

Tolya Valerik would have no great difficulty recognizing Death. Assuming he was home.

The doorman didn't bother questioning their errand, though he cast a pointed glance in the direction of a large clock mounted on the lobby wall. Presumably, he knew they weren't tenants, but his security function was limited to booting panhandlers and obvious ne'er-do-wells, calling police if he needed more serious backup. There would be trouble if they came back through the lobby with a television set or stereo, likewise if they made too much noise upstairs. But if the probe got rowdy, Bolan didn't plan to stick around and chat with the police, in French or any other language.

"That was seven?" Johnny asked, before he pushed the button to select their floor.

"Seven," the Executioner confirmed.

Glancing at the mirrors that surrounded them, Johnny remarked, "If we had shades, we'd look like Men in Black."

"The only Man in Black I know is Johnny Cash," Bolan replied.

"You're out of touch, bro. Sadly out of touch."

"It works for me."

They kept their weapons under cover on the short ride up, on the slim chance that somebody might be waiting for the elevator, somewhere in between the lobby and the seventh floor. It didn't happen, and the brothers drew their matching SMGs from beneath their coats as they left the car, then turned left along a silent hallway toward apartment 7G.

There were no guards outside the door, which could mean anything—or nothing. Standing side by side, in front of it, they listened for a moment, picking up the faint sounds of what might be television—yes, there was the laugh track—playing from inside.

"You want to ring the bell?" Johnny inquired.

"I'd rather not."

"Okay. On three, then?"

"Three it is."

JOHNNY WAS BUZZING as he got to "three" and gave the door a solid kick, above and slightly to the right of the knob. One should have done the trick, but it was solid, and he felt a sharp pain lance his ankle.

"Shit!"

He stepped back, lunged and slammed another kick into the stout, unyielding door, pain shooting through his foot and ankle.

"Jesus!"

"Blow it!"

Johnny hit the lock and doorknob with a burst of Parabellum hollowpoints. At point-blank range, the slugs lost none of their 1,300-feet-per-second muzzle velocity, ripping through wood and metal as if he had savaged the door with an electric saw. He kicked the door again—same pain in heel and shin—but this time it flew open and he followed through, his brother crowding close behind him.

They had given up whatever margin of surprise that might have once graced their venture. There were five or six guys in the living room, their jackets off and ties undone, watching some kind of lesbian porn tape on a giant-screen TV. Another target was in the kitchen, off to Johnny's left, where he appeared to be making popcorn. Hallways led away in both directions from the living room, all dark and silent now.

A trained observer, Johnny registered those facts almost unconsciously, while focused on the conduct of his mission. None of those now gawping at him was the man he sought, and Johnny raked the nearby sofa with a burst of automatic fire, saw bits and pieces disengage from skulls and faces as he cut a swath from left to right.

Despite the hour and their shock, however, the majority of Russian shooters in the room weren't so flabbergasted that they found themselves immobilized. The gunner in the kitchen had drawn a shiny autoloading pistol by the time they beat the stubborn door, and he got off two rounds before the Executioner hit him with a short burst to the chest. His bullets slapped into the wall and door frame, maybe five, six inches over Johnny's head, but it wasn't the near-miss that made Johnny curse and grimace.

No. It was the noise.

He reckoned that Valerik's neighbors may have slept through his explosive entrance to the flat, assuming they were all home and asleep. Night owls could be a problem when it came to busting doors, regardless of the MP-5's effective sound suppressor. But now that the gunner in the kitchen had cranked off two rounds from .45-caliber pistol. Their hopes of pulling off a silent probe were definitely shot to hell.

So be it, then, the younger Bolan thought. What did he have to lose?

A Russian gunner stepped in front of the TV, a short pump-action shotgun in his hands.

There was no time to hesitate. Johnny's reaction was mechanical, ingrained, a simple pivot toward the mark, not flinching as he stroked the trigger of his MP-5. He didn't even really have to aim. The weapon was an extension of himself from hours of practice, in and out of uniform. His Army Ranger training, combat in Grenada, and the private battles he had waged since his discharge from military service all combined to let him know when he had target acquisition.

Johnny's adversary danced a little as bullets ripped into his chest and shoulder, spinning him. At least one Parabellum slug got past him. The giant-screen TV imploded with a sound like someone shattering five hundred light bulbs all at once, and blew a smoke ring that enveloped Johnny's target as he fell.

Five down, and Johnny saw that there were still two functional defenders, one hunched behind a large recliner, while the second huddled in the shadow of a second sofa. Both of them were armed with handguns, blasting aimless shots in the direction of the door when they had nerve enough to risk it, never peeking out to spot their targets more precisely or determine if their rounds had found the mark.

Johnny was duckwalking around the nearer sofa, as his brother moved to silence the remaining shooter on their left. He still had no idea if there was anybody else in the apartment, or if they were simply wasting time, risking their lives to take out soldiers who would otherwise had posed no threat to Mack and Johnny, or their manhunt for Valerik.

Concentrate, goddammit!

He was peering out from cover when his target raised a hand above the couch and squeezed off two more shots, not bothering to aim. It was a poor defense, no planning or precision to it, but the gunner may have reckoned it would hold his enemies at bay, while someone else called for help. At this point, Johnny guessed, with five of their companions down and out, even police would be a welcome sight to the embattled Russians.

Johnny watched the gun hand drop out of sight and made his move, a creeping kind of progress. It was hard on knees and elbows, even on the deep-shag carpet, but he made it to the near end of the other couch without attracting fire—or any notice from his enemy.

He waited, lying on the floor, uncertain whether his brother's opponent had a shot at him or not. It made the short hairs bristle on his nape, but Johnny had enough things on his mind without surrendering to paranoia. He was waiting for the Russian hunkered down behind the couch to make a move, and when he did—

The *pop-pop* of his adversary's pistol galvanized him. Johnny scooted forward, lizard-style, to poke his head and MP-5 around the corner of the sofa. Suddenly, he found the Russian shooter staring at him, shoulders hunched, his gun arm hoisted well above the sofa cushions, rapid-firing toward the door.

The gunman tried to save himself, bring his pistol to bear on the immediate threat, but it was already too late. Johnny shot him in the face from six or seven feet, a muffled burst that sounded more like someone ripping sailcloth. Blood exploded from the ruined mess, spattering warm drops in Johnny's face, and he was quick to wipe it with his sleeve, thinking about disease, the threat of hepatitis, AIDS or God knew what.

A death cry from the far side of the room told him that his brother had finished with his opposition, but it wasn't time to leave the battle suite. Not yet. Before they bailed, the brothers had to check the other rooms, make sure Tolya Valerik wasn't hiding in a closet, maybe underneath a bed.

Bolan didn't speak aloud as Johnny rose to his feet. Swift hand gestures split the flat in two, Bolan checking out the left-hand corridor, while Johnny took the right. He nodded in response and turned away, proceeding toward whatever lay beyond the blood-splashed living room.

LAVRENTI MALENKOV was on the verge of climax when all hell broke loose in the parlor, where his soldiers were supposed to be enjoying vodka, junk food and assorted triple-X cassettes on the large-screen TV. The sixteen-year-old hooker crouched between his legs was an expert at her craft. Lavrenti was perhaps ten seconds from rewarding her enthusiastic efforts when the crack of gunfire brought him jerking upright on the king-sized waterbed.

The Russian scrambled for his nightstand, cursing, yanking out the top drawer, fingers scrabbling for the Skorpion machine pistol he kept hidden there. In fact, there were Skorpions in both nightstands. Malenkov was ready for anything, regardless of the state his enemies might find him in. When he had a machine pistol in each hand, the solid four-pound weight of them familiar, reassuring, he scooted out of bed.

Malenkov was naked, and he hated meeting anyone that way, but the thought of dropping either weapon, much less both of them, to grapple with his clothes wasn't worth the risk. He stood there for a moment, listening to pistol fire exploding from the living room. The Russian knew that he had only seconds left in which to make his choice.

"Get up!" he told the hooker, as her tousled head poked up beyond the far side of the water bed. "Get up and fetch my robe!"

"Do what?"

He let her see the pistols, their stubby muzzles pointed at her face, and she decided any further argument wouldn't be to her best advantage. Starting out on hands and knees, she made it to her feet a moment later. "Where?" she asked.

"Where *what?*"

"Where do you keep your precious robe?"

Lavrenti felt a sudden urge to strike her, club her with a pistol where she stood, but she would be no good to him unconscious. "In the closet, dammit! Where else would it be?"

"I don't live here, remember? How the hell should I know where—"

He lashed out at her with a bare foot as she passed, catching one luscious buttock with sufficient force to stagger her. The hooker glared at him but shut her mouth and hurried to the walk-in closet, where his jet-black velvet robe hung from a hook.

"This it?" she asked him, velvet trailing on the floor around her feet.

"Come on!"

She came back with the robe and helped him into it, the process complicated by Lavrenti's absolute refusal to let go of either pistol. Twice, the Skorpions' curved magazines snagged on the inside of the sleeves, but he felt better when the cool, soft velvet draped his body.

"Fasten the belt," he ordered.

"Yes, sir! Right away, sir!"

On the first attempt, she didn't close the robe completely, leaving him exposed in front. Lavrenti cursed her, and she made a small adjustment, tightening the sash around his waist.

"What do I do now?" she asked.

"Go back to bed," he said, and swung his right-hand weapon in a short, sharp arc against her skull. The hooker made a tiny squeaking sound and toppled back onto the waterbed.

The shooting in the living room had stopped, but that wasn't a good sign, necessarily, since he heard nothing from his men. If they were still alive, victorious, they should have been congratulating one another, cursing the intruders they had beaten, rushing back to check on Malenkov and get him out of there before police arrived.

Because there were no sounds at all, Malenkov knew that one of two bad things had happened. His men and the trespassers had either killed each other off, thus leaving him alone, or the invaders were victorious, and he was still at mortal risk. Would they take time to search the rest of the apartment for surviving targets, or would they be anxious to depart, aware that one or more of Malenkov's affluent neighbors would have summoned the police by now?

In either case, it was imperative that Malenkov get out of the apartment. There were outlawed drugs and firearms on the premises, who knew how many dead men, plus an unconscious teenaged prostitute. If all of that wasn't bad enough, his very presence in Quebec broke half a dozen laws, since Malenkov had skipped the tedium of customs, immigration, passports, visas and the like. He was illegal, in the full sense of the word, and if he fell into official hands, the very least he could expect was deportation back to Mother Russia—where the list of charges waiting for him ranged from rape and robbery to half a dozen murder counts.

He had to fight and get away. That much was clear.

The bedroom door was closed. How could he open it, with both hands full? Malenkov compromised, tucking the left-hand Skorpion into his right armpit just long enough to turn the knob and pull the door ajar. From there, it was a simple task to hook a toe around the edge and pull it open far enough for him to see along the hallway leading to the living room. No movement there, at first, though he could smell the pall of cordite hanging in the air.

Malenkov gasped and stepped back into shadow, as a silhouette appeared and started moving toward him, down the hallway. He couldn't make out the face, but it wasn't one of his men. His soldiers wouldn't tiptoe down the hall, as if afraid of waking him, when they had just been shooting off guns in the living room.

The Russian checked his Skorpions, made sure both safety switches had been disengaged. He would have one slim chance to do this right, and failure meant his death. The stranger creeping toward his room with such exaggerated stealth wasn't a lawman. The police took pride in shouting, kicking doors and toppling furniture. Police had no concept of self-control.

His time was running out. Malenkov knew it, even as he braced himself to make his move. He started counting down from five, and when he got to one, he lunged around the corner, firing both machine pistols and rushing toward his startled adversary with a high-pitched battle cry.

THE KEVLAR VEST saved Bolan's life. One moment, he was moving down the silent hallway toward an open bedroom door, his eyes picking out the supple leg and rounded buttocks of a naked woman sprawled on satin sheets, and then two automatic weapons cut loose on him from the doorway, virtually in his face. The bullets drummed against his chest and drove him backward, taking him down. He held on to the MP-5 by sheer willpower, but before he had a chance to use it, a figure hurdled him.

He spent a precious moment understanding that he was alive, apparently unharmed beyond the throbbing ache that gripped his ribs and sternum. Being shot through Kevlar felt a lot like being kicked or beaten. It would bruise, perhaps crack bones, but he would live to fight another day, because his would-be killer had not taken time to finish it. A quick burst to the head as he was passing by, and…

Bolan scrambled to his feet, biting his lip against the pain. Another day would have to wait until he finished this one, and he still had one live target to secure, at least. Was it Valerik? Had he been that close, only to let the bastard slip away again?

He wasn't clear yet!

Staccato gunfire from the living room told Bolan that the runner had encountered Johnny. Sudden urgency gave Bolan strength to power through the pain, legs pumping as he sprinted down the corridor to help his brother.

Too late.

When Bolan reached the living room, the door was standing open wide, his brother crouched behind a bullet-torn Barcalounger, firing toward the doorway with his MP-5.

"Got past me, dammit!" Johnny said, as he was scrambling to his feet.

"I'm on it!" Bolan snapped, already past him, ducking out into the hall. A quick glance either way, and Bolan caught a dark swirl to his left, just disappearing through a door that opened on the service stairs. He slowed on the approach.

There was a small window in the door, about chest-high, with wire mesh sandwiched between two panes of glass. He took a chance, peered through it, ready to recoil, but there was no one waiting for him on the other side. He edged through, held the door and stood still for a moment, listening.

The sound came from below him, bare feet slapping on concrete, accompanied by labored breathing. Bolan started down, taking the steps two at a time, incapable of moving silently *and* swiftly. Sacrificing stealth for speed, he closed the gap between himself and his determined quarry.

Bolan might have let the runner go, if he was certain that the man wasn't Tolya Valerik. As it was, the Russian *mafioso* had eluded Bolan twice already, and he couldn't bear to come this close again, allow him to escape once more, unless he did his utmost to prevent it.

At the fifth-floor landing, Bolan nearly bought it. He was well into the turn, with one hand on the metal railing, when he saw his enemy at the bottom of the flight. A hasty glance showed him the Russian wore some kind of robe, but it had fallen open to expose his nakedness. He had an automatic weapon in each hand, already firing as the Executioner came into range, but Bolan caught another break. As bullets ricocheted around him, the soldier felt his right foot slipping on the stairs and took advantage of it, hauling on the rail, wrenching himself around toward something that at least resembled cover.

How many rounds were left in his enemy's weapons? They looked like Model 61 Skorpions, twenty rounds apiece, unless the Russian had some kind of special extended magazines. It was the third time he had fired, both guns together, with an average cyclic rate of 840 rounds per minute. Almost empty, then, and even if he had spare clips stashed in the pockets of his flapping robe, reloading would take time he didn't have.

Unless he scored a hit on Bolan first.

Wild rounds were striking sparks on impact with the metal railing, slivers stinging Bolan's face and scalp. He tried to roll away and felt a bullet strike his boot heel, while another traced a white-hot line across his thigh. Too close for comfort, and if the bastard didn't run dry soon...

There was a sharp metallic click below him, as one Skorpion's firing pin came down on an empty chamber. Knowing he couldn't afford to waste the moment, Bolan swung his legs around and lunged back toward the landing, sliding on his belly, with the MP-5 in front of him.

Downrange, the Russian dropped his empty weapon, wincing as it struck his shin, and thrust the other out in front of him, two-handed. Was it empty? Bolan couldn't take the chance.

He triggered a short burst from his SMG and watched the Russian stagger, one leg folding as he went down on his backside, swaddled in the jet-black robe. His Skorpion spit six or seven rounds before the slide locked open, but the shots were wasted, rattling over Bolan's head.

The Executioner rose and started down the stairs, the Russian sprawled below, his pale, lean body smeared with blood, the robe spread out beneath him like the dark wings of a dying bat. A sound of footsteps on the stairs, rapidly descending, made the warrior hesitate until he recognized his brother.

"Are you all right?" Johnny asked.

Bolan pressed an open palm against his thigh and checked the bleeding. "Just a graze," he said. "It's nothing."

"And it's not Valerik."

They were operating from an old surveillance photograph, but it was obvious. Tolya Valerik had an oval, meaty face.

The pallid visage Bolan saw before him now was long, with high cheekbones. Some women might have called it handsome, under better circumstances.

"Maybe he can tell us something," Bolan said. He crouched beside the almost-dead man, careful not to touch him. When the eyes swam into focus on his face, he said, "Tolya Valerik. Is he still in Montreal?"

No answer.

"We can call an ambulance," he said. "It may not be too late."

The Russian's grimace showed that he was still alert enough to recognize a lie. "F-f-f-f—"

"What's he saying?" Johnny asked.

Bolan leaned closer, watchful of the Russian's empty hands. He didn't need to have an eye snatched out by some last reflex of a dying enemy.

"Try harder," he suggested.

"F-f-f-f—"

"He's losing it," Johnny remarked. "He's gone."

"Fuck you, American."

And then he was gone, blue eyes glazing over, dying with a vague smile on his face.

"I guess he told you," Johnny said.

"I guess he did."

2

Tolya Valerik lit a fresh cigarette from the stub of his last and drew the sweet smoke deep into his lungs. He washed it down with vodka, hoping that the mix of alcohol and nicotine would calm him, but it failed to quell the buzzing in his head, a low-pitched sound that brought to mind defective neon lights. The noise was only in his mind, Valerik realized, but he had checked the room's light fixtures, just in case.

"They've followed us," he said.

Anatoly Bogdashka, his second in command, frowned. "We don't know that for sure," he said.

"Lavrenti Malenkov and seven of his men—my men—are dead!" Valerik snapped. "You think that is a coincidence, after the bloody business in New York and California?"

"Not coincidence, of course," Bogdashka said, clearly aware he was treading shaky ground. "But maybe not the same men, either. We don't know who killed Lavrenti and the rest."

"We don't know anything, goddammit! That's the trouble. We're supposed to have 'intelligence,' our so-called friends are such great experts, and they shrug like stupid children when I ask them for opinions. Idiots!"

"Lavrenti was expecting trouble with the Triads," Bogdashka offered. "You remember that, of course. The heroin connection into Montreal. With these Chinese—"

Valerik interrupted him. "Are you forgetting that the doorman saw Lavrenti's killers? They were white men, Anatoly, not Chinese.''

"Perhaps contract assassins?" From his tone, Valerik understood that Bogdashka didn't buy it. He was simply playing devil's advocate, or maybe trying to relieve his boss of some anxiety.

"The same men, Anatoly. Mark my words." He saw Bogdashka's frown and said, "You think I'm being paranoid?"

"Of course not, Tolya. Someone obviously has a killing grudge against our Family. I simply wonder how these people came to know we were in Quebec."

How, indeed? Valerik asked himself. How had the bastards tracked him from Los Angeles to New York City? How had they managed to infiltrate and destroy his private retreat on Long Island?

"We could answer that," he said, "if we knew who they were. What does our friend at Langley have to say?"

"'I'm working on it,'" Bogdashka mimicked Noble Pruett's voice, exaggerating the speech impediment that lingered from an infantile cleft palate. "He knows nothing, but pretends that he is on the brink of some great revelation. It's a lawman's trick. They do it all the time."

"You think he's trying, though?"

Bogdashka shrugged. "Why wouldn't he? It's his game, too. He has as much to lose as anyone. Unless—"

Valerik raised a hand to silence his lieutenant. "I've considered the alternative," he said. "If he was working for the other side, to set us up, we'd all have been in jail a year ago. And all this killing? No. It makes no sense."

Another shrug. "He's clumsy, then. Not worth his paycheck as a spy."

"Or overmatched, perhaps."

"Why's that?" Bogdashka looked confused.

"Nothing." Valerik waved it off. "The men who killed Lavrenti made no mention of a Billy King?"

"Who knows? The two of them said nothing to the doorman. No one else who saw them is alive." Bogdashka paused, then said, "You're thinking of New York again."

"And California."

Less than two weeks ago, the name of Billy King had meant nothing to Valerik. Blissful ignorance had masked the approaching nightmare that now threatened to jeopardize his empire, his very life itself.

This day, Valerik was haunted by the name of a pathetic small-time criminal whom he had never met, a man already dead before Valerik learned that he had ever lived. As the Russian understood it, King had been employed by one of Noble Pruett's contract agents named Ted Williams. He was someone who could handle scut work with a fair degree of competency and a minimum of whining. It had been a poor selection; King had overreached himself and tried to steal from stronger, wiser men in the belief that he wouldn't be caught. Of course, he was caught, and had been eliminated as a matter of routine.

It was the kind of housecleaning detail that Valerik's field commanders handled on their own, without consulting headquarters. Who cared if some American ex-convict with a record dating from his adolescent years dropped out of sight? Good riddance to bad rubbish, as the Yanks would say.

Apparently, however, there was one who cared. King's older sister, Suzanne, loved her worthless sibling, God alone knew why, and she had made inquiries. When authorities in San Diego demonstrated no concern for her brother's whereabouts—perhaps relieved that he had left their jurisdiction, hoping he wouldn't return—Suzanne King had employed a private investigator.

His name was Johnny Gray.

It was at that point, only nine days earlier, that Valerik heard of Billy King for the first time. He wasn't overly concerned about the sister and her "private dick," but he had moved to silence them on general principle, believing—as experience had taught him—that his interests were best served by weeding out potential enemies before they knew enough or had sufficient strength to threaten him. Again, it was routine, like swatting insects.

But the sister and her sleuth-for-hire had stubbornly refused to die. In fact, when Valerik's soldiers cornered them in Arizona, on their way to question one of Pruett's flunkies, they had killed a number of his men and slipped away, apparently unscathed. Noble Pruett had sent one of his men with Bogdashka's killers to silence the CIA connection, but they had arrived too late. Their target, Ted Williams—if the name could be believed—was dead when they arrived, an apparent suicide. Pruett suspected he had been interrogated first, perhaps by Suzanne King and her detective. As to how the link was made, the man from Langley had no clue.

And things had gone downhill from there. Within twenty-four hours of the Tucson fiasco, unknown gunmen had begun attacking Valerik's enterprises in Los Angeles. At each location where they struck, survivors had been left with questions about Billy King, an implication that the assaults would continue until King was produced, or his whereabouts revealed.

Valerik and Bogdashka had left Los Angeles five days earlier, seeking refuge in Manhattan. And somehow, before another day was out, the bloodshed had resumed, this time in New York City. Once again, the raiders made a point of naming Billy King, although, as far as Valerik could discover, King had never traveled any farther east than Arizona. It was wasted effort, if his adversaries truly wished to find the missing felon, but they had disrupted the Russian's operations in New York—the flagship of his empire in the States—and forced him to evacuate the country with a daring raid against his safe house on Long Island.

Now, the bastards seemingly had trailed him to Quebec. The mayhem had begun again.

Lavrenti Malenkov had been a friend of Valerik's from the old days when they ran the Moscow streets together, stealing, mugging drunks and dodging the military patrols. They had been good at it, enjoyed the sport as much as the profits, though no one was perfect. They hadn't always managed to escape. Both had been caged and beaten on occasion, as young "enemies of the people," and both had been "reeducated" as adults. In fact, the only thing they learned had been new ways to beat the system, up until the moment when the system had surprised them and collapsed. By that time, they were wealthy men, with reputations to be feared. The sudden death of communism simply gave Valerik and his kind a chance to show it off more openly.

He had selected Malenkov to head the Family business in Quebec because Malenkov spoke fluent French and because he was totally ruthless. There were forces already in place— the competitive Chinese, the scheming Corsicans—who would have happily devoured a softer man. Malenkov never shied away from wet work when it served the Family, but he wasn't a wild man, either. He knew how to strike the proper balance between diplomacy and force. He could negotiate, as well as kill.

Neither technique had served him well the previous night, apparently, though from the information that Valerik had received, Malenkov had resisted death, nearly escaped the trap.

Nearly escaped. It was a stupid phrase, like "slightly pregnant," or "presumed innocent." The only thing that really mattered was the ultimate result. One either managed to escape a trap, or one didn't. Those who didn't were caged or killed. There was no middle ground, no last-ditch consolation prize for those who almost got away, then stumbled near the finish line.

Tolya Valerik did not grieve for Malenkov. He missed his

childhood friend, of course, experienced a mix of anger and sadness at the thought of never seeing Malenkov again, but the same emotional deficit that made him a consummate thief and killer prevented Valerik from truly grieving over anyone. Although he didn't read psychology, wasn't acquainted with the latest terminology, he likely would have recognized himself in textbook descriptions of something called "antisocial personality disorder." APD was a relatively new buzz word in the field of mental health, adopted in the age of creeping political correctness to replace an older, more "prejudicial" term.

A few years earlier, psychologists would have labeled Valerik a sociopath. A few years before that, they would have called him a psychopath. It all came down to one thing in the end: a human predator devoid of what society called "conscience," self-centered to the point where other human beings were objectified, evaluated and manipulated—or eliminated—on the basis of their bottom-line worth to Number One.

If he had bothered to peruse the textbooks, Valerik would have known himself on sight, and he wouldn't have disagreed with the description. Nothing in the classic texts would have offended him—nor would it have influenced him to change. Why should he, when his personality "disorder" placed the whole world at his very fingertips?

"I have to speak with Krestyanov," Valerik said. He had been trying to postpone the moment, but he couldn't put it off any longer. Better to be done with it, deliver the bad news—the new bad news—than to delay and make it that much worse. Valerik had no way of knowing when or where his unknown nemesis would strike again, but if the past ten days had taught him anything, the lesson had to be that they—whoever they were—had a grim, relentless taste for blood.

Not so unlike his own.

"He won't be pleased," Bogdashka said.

"When is he?"

Bogdashka laughed at that and drained his glass of vodka. "Anyway," he said, "it was a smart move not to stay at the apartment."

Valerik had decided on the smaller flat in Mont-Royal, a whim as much as any rational consideration, and his luck had served him for the first time during recent days. It could, he realized, as easily have gone the other way. He could be lying on a steel bed, in a small refrigerated drawer, gut shot.

Better it should happen to a friend, he thought, and felt no passing qualms of guilt. Survival was nothing to be ashamed of. Truth be told, it was the only proved virtue in Valerik's world. The only thing he trusted, next to money.

Krestyanov would be displeased, indeed, but that couldn't be helped. Valerik had already recognized what he had to do to save himself, his Family. He should have done it after the fiasco on Long Island, but he had allowed himself to be convinced by Krestyanov that he would be safe in Canada, more readily available to make command decisions and assist with any problems in the States. As it turned out, the problems in the States had followed him to Montreal and roosted on his very doorstep. Now, at last, he meant to put himself beyond the reach of his relentless enemies.Where he could make the rules. Krestyanov might object, but that was his problem. He wasn't the one who had been losing soldiers, money, property and precious anonymity, as if his once-charmed life had suddenly become the object of an evil curse.

As for the trouble in America, Valerik would leave it to Americans. Let Pruett earn his money for a change, instead of simply smirking, making vague allusions to his "pull" and "weight." The time had come for the CIA man to throw some of that weight around and pull them all out of the unexpected tar pit that was sucking at their feet.

Valerik flicked a hateful glance in the direction of the telephone, and Bogdashka took the cue. "I should be checking in with our man at the Royal Mounted Police," he explained, rising to leave. "There may be something new about Lavrenti."

"I suspect you'll find that he's still dead," Valerik said.

VASSILY KRESTYANOV was a survivor. In his lifetime, he had weathered many storms and bulled his way past two great tragedies. Nietzsche once had written that whatever didn't kill him made him stronger. Krestyanov wouldn't have been surprised to learn the slogan had been plagiarized from some forgotten child of Mother Russia.

The first great tragedy of Krestyanov's life had occurred in 1982. At that time, he was already thirty years old, a captain in the KGB who kept his nose clean, more or less, eyes fixed on the promotion track. His parents were deceased, and he had lost his only brother to a land mine in Afghanistan. such incidents were troubles, but they weren't tragedies, in Krestyanov's perception. Death and loss were part of normal life. A tragedy, by contrast, he defined as an event that could derail his life, imperil his career.

The day he learned his wife was fucking an American reporter from *The New York Times,* Vassily Krestyanov had seen his whole life flash before his eyes. Whatever private rage or jealousy he felt was nothing by comparison to his concern for what would happen if some other up-and-comer at Dzerzhinsky Square should stumble on Marina's indiscretion and report him as the husband of a traitor, possibly himself a double agent for the hated CIA. Krestyanov knew the way things worked, once the machine was set in motion. By the time they finished with him, torturing him nonstop in the basement of the Lubyanka prison, Krestyanov would certainly confess to spying for America. By then, he knew, it was entirely possible he would believe the charge himself.

There was but one solution to the problem, as he worked

it out. Clearly, Marina's crime couldn't be tolerated or ignored. Killing his wife and/or her twenty-something stud wouldn't resolve the problem, either, since the link between them could be found posthumously, connections made through witnesses and paper trails. The one and only road to personal salvation had been crystal clear, albeit not without some latent danger to himself.

Krestyanov had denounced Marina and her lover to his colonel, who—after recovering from his initial shock—had passed the information on. When it was time for the arrest, he led the team to lift Marina from her tiny secretary's office. Krestyanov could still recall the moment, her surprise, the fleeting smile that vanished like a small mirage when she was made to understand that he wasn't inviting her to lunch. Krestyanov had participated in his wife's interrogation at the Lubyanka, typed up her confession with his own two hands and testified against her as the leading prosecution witness at Marina's trial. When she was packed off for reeducation at Kirovsk, he waited for the other shoe to drop.

And was promoted, six weeks later, to the rank of major.

Tragedy had been averted. Private justice had been served.

The second tragedy in Vassily Krestyanov's life had occurred on August 29, 1991, when the Soviet Parliament voted to suspend all activities of the Communist Party. The Soviet Union itself had disintegrated four months later, on December 26, and the KGB had gone with it—in name, at least. Old tactics were renounced, at least in public, and he found their private use increasingly proscribed in the name of democracy. As the Russian economy foundered, civil wars erupting in the satellite republics, only criminal pursuits appeared to prosper.

Krestyanov had yet another choice to make, and there had been no hesitation. He had seen the warning signs far in advance and had prepared himself to cut his losses. If his own wife had no final claim upon his loyalty, what hope did fat-assed politicians have?

On balance—until very recently, at least—Krestyanov thought that he had made the wise choice, going private when he did. His KGB connections served him well, both in connecting to the Russian underworld and in facilitating acquisition of those Russian products that would bring the highest price abroad. Krestyanov's stock-in-trade included various commodities, from simple bits of information to sophisticated military hardware. He was doing very well indeed, financially.

And yet...

The truth was that he missed the old days.

Krestyanov would never be mistaken for a sentimental man. He didn't wax nostalgic for the "worker's paradise" of communism, since no such Utopia had ever existed. Instead, he missed the sense of order—illusory though it may have been, at times—that had vanished when the USSR collapsed. He missed the cold war, with its enemies and allies. More than anything, he missed the grim, iron-muscled state that had known how to keep all its rebels and riffraff in line.

Unlike most men who looked back fondly on the "good old days," however, Krestyanov had actually devised a way to bring them back. It seemed to him an almost foolproof plan.

Almost.

He had been suffering from doubt, these days. Not of his own performance, or the planning he had done, but rather of the allies he had chosen. The Americans, despite their evident enthusiasm, were cautious almost to the point of inactivity. Noble Pruett, Krestyanov's "opposite number," as it were, came equipped with a laundry list of domestic hazards that eternally prevented him from taking a too-active role in the United States. Pruett worried about the CIA charter, the White House, the FBI, Internal Revenue, congressional oversight committees, the press, state and local police, the fear of "getting caught with his pants down."

In the beginning, Krestyanov had thought Tolya Valerik would turn out to be the stronger of his allies, motivated more by honest greed than by any illusory concept such as patriotism. Valerik and his soldiers got things done. They were adept at solving problems, and it didn't bother Krestyanov that violence was often their first resort, instead of the last. It was a methodology he could respect, and one that he had frequently employed, himself, while working for the KGB.

But something had gone wrong somewhere along the way. Krestyanov didn't fully understand the details, some nonsense about a woman looking for her brother, hiring a detective to assist her in the search. There were no "private eyes" in Russia, where citizens were accustomed to having their every move watched by the state. Krestyanov grasped the concept of consulting detectives, understood their techniques, more or less, and knew their kind had been romanticized beyond all reason in America. What he could not grasp was the quantum leap from one or two investigators, working on a missing-person case, to all-out war between Tolya Valerik and some well-armed, nameless enemy who struck at will, across the continent, endangering Krestyanov's precious brainchild in the process.

His disappointment in Valerik was a given. Valerik should have crushed his adversaries, during their initial moves against him. To prolong the conflict, let it rage from coast to coast—now slopping into Canada—was unforgivable. Some fitting punishment would have to be devised for Valerik if he managed to survive, but now wasn't the time. Their only hope of salvaging the situation lay in solidarity. Perhaps, all things considered, it was best that Valerik leave the country after all.

Krestyanov could have moved to prevent it, either through negotiation or some harsher method, but the more he thought about it, Valerik's plan appeared to have some merit. Since his operations were the focus of attacks in California, New York and Quebec, there was at least a fifty-fifty chance that his removal from the scene would bring about a unilateral cease-fire. Conversely, if his enemies persisted, they would have to pack their guns and head for Europe. Either way, the stateside preparations for their *konspiratsia* would be resumed, without further interference from persons unknown.

Valerik could look after himself in Europe, while nailing down the final details of the plan on that front, moving the material and men they would require to see it through.

And Pruett could begin to earn his keep at home, instead of sitting on his hands.

All this had come together in Krestyanov's mind while he was on the telephone with Valerik, moments earlier. He had already known about the deaths in Montreal and wouldn't be surprised if there were more to come. Valerik had been startled and relieved when Krestyanov agreed to his evacuation without protest. Clearly, he had been expecting Krestyanov to offer some objection, maybe fly into a fit of rage or whine and plead with him to stay.

On second thought, no man who knew Vassily Krestyanov for any length of time would ever look for him to whine and beg. It wasn't in his nature any more than praying to imaginary gods or finding his erotic pleasures in the company of men. Vassily Krestyanov would die before he begged a living soul for anything, and he had no intention of dying for a long, long time.

As for his enemies…well, that would be a different story. Some of them were dead already; others would inevitably follow, as his grand design took shape. The men who had abandoned and betrayed their homeland, who had dishonored the sacrifice of countless heroes for the wet dream of Westernization, would be forced to deal with Krestyanov when he came into his own.

Of course, by then, it would be too late for any deals.

There would be only scorched earth for the traitors. Nothing left for them but cold and lonely graves.

The change on Pruett's end, in the United States, wouldn't be so dramatic. The Americans had quaint ideas concerning power and its naked exercise. They still toyed with the fiction spawned in Philadelphia, more than two hundred years ago, that spoke about "government of the people, by the people, for the people."

The very notion brought a smile to Vassily Krestyanov's rugged face.

There had never, in all of human history, existed a government "by the people, for the people." It was an impossibility, as far as Krestyanov could tell—a brief but concise description of primitive Utopian communism. In practice, *all* governments, regardless of their politics and posing, came down to a case of the few ruling many, wielding power for their own benefit, more often than not. It was the same story everywhere. Some states were more humane than others, some were less corrupt than usual, but none were truly governed by "the people."

Vassily Krestyanov didn't concern himself with whether any given government was "fair," its leadership corrupt or relatively "clean." What truly mattered was the end result, whether the state provided order and security at home—the only true foundation for prosperity—and kept its national defenses strong, repelling sundry enemies. All else was window dressing, a charade required by certain hypocrites before they could enjoy the game of dominating their inferiors.

Ends *always* justified the means. It was a law of nature, as immutable as gravity and death itself.

When Krestyanov and his associates were finally victorious, order would be restored. It might not be apparent to the casual observer, but there would be a balance to the world that had been sadly lacking for the best part of a decade.

Some would have to suffer, even die, before that vision was transformed into reality.

So what?

If it was any other way, "the people" would dissolve into a snarling pack of savages, their only rule survival of the fittest. And the strong would still prevail, albeit at a vastly greater cost to lives and property.

In Krestyanov's mind, his plan was not only the best solution, it was the only possible solution, short of global chaos.

He hoped Tolya Valerik and his entourage would have a safe and uneventful transatlantic flight. The sooner they were tucked away in Europe, now, the better Krestyanov would like it. There was still much work remaining to be done on both fronts, and the thugs wouldn't be idle.

He would personally see to that.

And in the meantime, Krestyanov would have a word with Noble Pruett, to remind him that success demanded full cooperation, each and every member of the team contributing 110 percent of concentration. Krestyanov demanded no less of himself, and he wasn't about to let his allies coast, while he did all the work.

Someone had to crack the whip.

And Krestyanov had always loved the way the whip felt in his hand.

At 8:15 a.m. on Thursday, Barbara Price was plotting murder over scrambled eggs and bacon.

She didn't intend to kill the chef.

Somewhere in Thailand, possibly in Laos or Burma, there was a man named Nong Sawan, age thirty-seven, who controlled a private army of some six or seven thousand men. He was a bandit, smuggler, narco-trafficker and terrorist, whose latest get-rich scheme involved the resurrection of a heroin empire that had been crippled twelve months earlier by the retirement of an aging warlord in the Golden Triangle. The powers that be in Washington were bent on stopping Sawan by any means available, and Hal Brognola had assigned the planning phase of the attack to Barbara Price, in her role as mission controller at Stony Man Farm.

She would assign Phoenix Force. Play the game by ear, once they were on the ground in Bangkok, hoping for a lead to Sawan that would permit them to achieve desired results. It would be dicey, but the team was used to that. The Phoenix Force warriors seemed to thrive on danger, caring only that the ultimate reward was worth the risk involved. This time around—

The chiming telephone distracted her. All calls to the Farm came through a switchboard that was manned around the clock, and every telephone was fitted with a scrambler, each line tested once a week, on average, to make sure it was secure.

"Price," she said into the mouthpiece, flicking crumbs of toast with her free hand.

"You have a call from Striker, ma'am," the operator said.

Her heart lurched, rose into her throat. She spoke around it.

"Patch him through."

A deep, familiar voice came on the line. "How are the scrambled eggs?"

The automatic smile was painful, heavy on her face. "Are you saying I'm predictable?"

"That wouldn't be my word," Bolan replied. "How are you, Barbara?"

"I'm keeping busy." No specifics. There were no such things as social calls to Stony Man. "Yourself?"

"I need some information," Bolan said, "ASAP."

And there it was. The moment she had dreaded since her final argument with Hal Brognola. Bolan was calling, asking, and she had her orders. There was no way she could "accidentally" mistake or misinterpret what she had been told to do.

Bare minimum. Brognola's words. The basic who and where, with no specifics. Field support was unavailable.

"What information would that be?" she asked.

The silence on the other end was no more than a heartbeat long, but it still registered. "I don't know if Hal told you what I'm working on," he said.

"Bare bones," she lied. The big Fed had described a good deal more than that, although she knew that he was holding back. The *what* had troubled Price far less than the *why*. "The Russian Mob, he said."

Another fleeting hesitation. She could feel him weighing her response, dissecting it, a verbal autopsy. "He mention any names?"

"Tolya Valerik," she acknowledged, following the script. "A fairly major player out of Moscow, operating in the

States part-time since '95 or '96. He's got his sticky fingers in a hundred different pies.'' She hesitated, then went on. "I understand this is a private missing-person thing.''

"It started out that way," Bolan said. "At the moment, I'm not sure exactly what it is.''

"Where are you?" Price asked. She knew the answer—knew where he had been at midnight, anyway—and asked the question, wondering if he would lie. If it had gone that far.

"In Montreal," he said. She would confirm it with the switchboard later, on the caller ID box. "We missed Valerik.''

We. That told her he was still with Johnny, still on the scent. It didn't surprise her. The brothers were two of a kind.

"I'm sorry." She held back from adding that you didn't kill him. It was understood between them that the Executioner didn't intend to simply watch Valerik, tap his telephones or make a citizen's arrest.

"We checked out two other places," Bolan said, "but he's given us the slip again.''

She pictured the soldier's features as he spoke, the grim set of his jaw, eyes that could smolder, then go frosty in an instant, making target acquisition. She had seen his war face, and the other one, as well.

"You need to get a line on him." She didn't phrase it as a question. What would be the point? Bolan wasn't calling to discuss the yearly rainfall in the Blue Ridge Mountains, where the Farm was situated.

"That would help," he said. "If there's a problem, though…''

He left it hanging, wouldn't spell it out, uncertain as to whether she was conscious of the rift between himself and Brognola. To broach the subject, if she didn't know, would only make things worse, perhaps torpedo any chance he had of gleaning information on the sly. And if she did know, if she had already chosen sides, whatever comments Bolan made would be redundant, simply wasted breath.

"You caught a break," she told him, trying to sound cheerful. Selling it. "We show him outbound from Quebec at 5:30 a.m., your time, with two companions, on a nonstop flight to Amsterdam."

In the ensuing silence, she could picture Bolan thinking through the choice of destinations. Why not London, Paris, Rome or even Moscow? Was Valerik bound for home by some diversionary route, or was he simply looking for a place to hide?

"That's interesting," he said at last. "I don't suppose you have a more specific fix on where he's going?"

"Sorry, no," she said. That much was true, at least. So far. If she learned more, then Price knew that she would have a painful choice to make.

Divided loyalties were a bitch.

"Okay," the soldier said. "Thanks, anyway."

He was about to go, her mind's eye saw him cradling the telephone, but Price didn't want to lose him yet. She was oppressed by a sensation that she might not hear his voice again, might never see the smile that changed his solemn face so radically.

"How are you holding up?" she asked, and grimaced at the way it came out sounding trite, a sad cliché.

"I'm holding," Bolan said. He left it there.

"And Johnny?" Christ! she thought. Why didn't she ask him if it looked like rain?

"He's good," Bolan said. "He makes me proud."

It was so unexpected—not the sentiment; the spoken words—that Price was taken by surprise. She felt a need to answer him somehow, and settled for, "It must run in the family."

Oh, God.

The words had barely passed her lips when Price realized

how they had to sound, recalling Bolan's family tragedy, the shooting that had left his parents and his younger sister dead, before he launched his one-man war against the Mafia in Massachusetts.

Bolan, for his part, either failed to notice the faux pas or simply let it pass. "I don't know about that," was all he said.

"You're watching out for each other?" Price asked. It was a clumsy rebound from her last gaffe, but Bolan didn't seem to pick up on her sudden lapse in conversation skills.

"We're doing all right, so far," he replied. "Hear much from Hal these days?"

Her conscious mind kicked into Defcon 4, which triggered automatic guilt feelings, a tightness in her chest.

Bolan and Brognola were at odds for the first time in her experience, and while she didn't understand precisely why this Russian business had divided them, she found herself caught in the middle once again. Brognola ran the show at Stony Man. He called the shots. Bolan, on the other hand, had been encouraged and conditioned to regard the Farm as a lifeline of sorts, a conduit for battlefield intelligence, advice and technical support, hardware, and reinforcements on those rare occasions when he needed backup in the field.

Brognola's "bare minimum" order had changed all that, his stony silence in response to Price's questions leaving a critical gap. She understood that something was wrong between the two most important men in her life, but she didn't know what, and that left her floundering, critically distracted from the daily life-or-death decisions of her job.

It also made her lie.

"He's jammed up pretty good these days in Wonderland," she said, using their standard label for the nation's capital. "It's been a couple weeks since he came down to see us."

The momentary silence on his end condemned her. She condemned herself.

Liar!

Brognola had last visited the Farm on Monday afternoon, issuing orders he regarded as too sensitive for the scrambled telephone lines. No explanations, just orders. When he left, unanswered questions trailing in his wake, it felt as if he had infected all those present with a virus whose symptoms included paranoia and guilt.

"I guess he's got his hands full," Bolan said. There was a certain distance to his voice. She felt a sudden chill, as if the air-conditioning had just kicked in.

"It's always something. You know Hal."

"I'll be in touch," Bolan said icily, and severed the connection.

Price sat still for several seconds, the dial tone humming in her ear, before she cradled the receiver. Next, she pushed her breakfast plate aside, as far away from her as she could reach without rising from her seat. Her appetite was gone, replaced by visceral anxiety.

The all-new Tension Diet, the mission controller thought, a bitter smile tugging at the corners of her mouth. She could tape an infomercial and buy time on late-night television, maybe clear a bundle from neurotics who would pay to learn how their misgivings could be used to trim their waistlines.

It was so damned funny, she forgot to laugh.

The hell of it was that she couldn't think of any way to heal the breach between Brognola and his single most important agent in the field, not knowing what it was. Brognola didn't want Bolan on the Russian job, that much was clear, but he had left her without any cogent explanation for his strange—indeed, unprecedented—attitude.

And it got worse. Brognola had left orders that he be informed if Bolan got in touch with anyone at Stony Man, for any reason whatsoever. He had stopped short of demanding transcripts of the calls, perhaps uncertain whether there would be any, but all incoming calls were automatically recorded, with the tapes erased at weekly intervals, except for "special" calls that might remain on file for years. Outgoing calls were clear, unless the person dialing out took special steps to have the conversation taped.

Now, Price had a call to make, and she was dreading it. It would compound her lies to Bolan, making the betrayal that much worse. She wasn't only holding back on information that he needed and denying the same, but now she had to run around behind his back, reporting on him to Brognola like some tattletale in grade school. That, in turn, brought Price's pangs of guilt back at full-force.

Where did her loyalties lie? Who would she choose if it came down to that?

A week ago, the very question would have been unthinkable. Brognola and the Executioner had been two fingers on the same strong hand.

And there was nothing she could do.

It was Brognola's job to hold the team together and transmit their orders from the highest levels. Their program was so secret, knowledge of its missions—its very existence—so tightly restricted that there had been no previous need for secrets inside the shop. She knew what Aaron Kurtzman and the others knew, because they signed off on the same reports and memos, sat through the same briefings and brainstormed their problems together like a study group in med school. She could plot the moves of Able Team and Phoenix Force no matter where they were on Earth, regardless of their task, and she knew where to reach them, more or less, when they weren't engaged. She had Brognola's private numbers and had learned to read his moods. Sometimes, she almost thought that she could read his mind.

But not this time.

Brognola's friendship with the Executioner had been cemented long before she came aboard—before there was a team to join, in fact. It had been one-on-one when Bolan worked the mean streets by himself, giving the Mafia a taste of hell on earth. If anyone had asked her, ten short days ago, Price would have said it was impossible for anything to break that bond of trust.

And she would have been wrong.

Disgusted with herself, she lifted the receiver and tapped in Brognola's office number. It rang three times, and Price had decided she would give up after four, her duty done, when the big Fed picked up.

"Brognola." Was the man as weary as he sounded, or was she projecting her own emotional fatigue?

"It's me," she said, and closed her eyes. "We got a call."

"SO, WHAT'S IN Amsterdam?" Suzanne King asked.

She sat with Johnny on the bed in her hotel room, daylight visible between them, to avoid the inference that they were somehow linked, involved beyond the physical requirements of the mission. Bolan knew the truth, and while it troubled him, he kept the observation to himself. His brother was a grown man and a blooded soldier. He couldn't be chastised like some kid in junior high for holding hands and sneaking kisses out behind the gym.

Not even if it cost his life.

"It could be anything," Bolan replied to Suzanne's question.

"Amsterdam's the flesh market of Western Europe. Same for drugs. The laws are lax, where they exist at all. It's known the Russian Mafia moves prostitutes and contraband through Amsterdam to London, Paris, Rome, Berlin, and on to North America. They've got their hooks into the red-light district and the local narcotraffic, too. It's Europe's version of the 'open city,' like Las Vegas and Miami for the stateside syndicate. Valerik will have people there. He may think it's a good place to drop out of sight."

"But we won't let him, right?" Her tone was filled with

grim determination and eagerness. "I mean, we can't just let him get away."

Twice with the "we." Johnny had marked her choice of words, as well, but he remained impassive, silent. Bolan steeled himself for what could be an ugly scene.

"Suzanne—"

"I know my brother's dead, okay?" The words stopped Bolan cold. "I still can't prove it, but I know. I'm not hallucinating that he may pop up in Europe, somewhere, riding in a gondola or fishing off London Bridge. You need to understand that I'm in touch with that reality."

No tears, despite the tension in her voice. It was a start.

"In that case," Bolan said, "you also understand that there's no reason for you to come with us to Amsterdam. You never met Valerik or the others. You can't help us run them down or—"

"Kill them," Suzanne finished for him. "I've got nothing to contribute, is your message. Worse than that, if I went with you, I'd get in the way and slow you down."

"It's nothing personal," he told her, "but you're absolutely right. You're not a soldier. This is killing work, no prisoners. I promise, you don't *want* to be there."

"Wrong." She faced him squarely, unyielding. "These bastards killed my brother, or they had it done. They tried to kill me, back at that motel in Arizona. Now, you may say that's no reason to pursue them—"

"It's a perfect reason," Bolan interrupted her, "but you don't have the skills to pull it off. Leave it to the professionals."

"Meaning the two of you," she said, and glanced at Johnny, seated by her side.

"That's right," Bolan said.

"Fair enough," she replied. "I'm not a soldier. There's no argument on that score, even though I'd say I held my end up pretty well, the night they tried to kill us."

"No one's saying you're incompetent, Suzanne." The comment came from Johnny, unaccustomed color rising in his cheeks. "You'll admit there's a big difference, though, between fighting when you're cornered and planning an attack on killers who outnumber you fifty, maybe a hundred to one."

She nodded. "Absolutely. I'm not asking you to give me a machine gun and a place in the front lines. I don't confuse myself with G.I. Jane."

"What, then?" Bolan asked.

"Just an answer to one simple question," she replied. "While you're both off in Amsterdam or God knows where, who's looking after me?"

Her voice lost volume as she asked the question, and her shoulders slumped a little. It was costing her, Bolan could tell, to speak of private weakness and acknowledge fear. He caught his brother staring at him, was still searching for the proper words to say, when Suzanne spoke again.

"I mean, they haven't given up on killing me, as far as I can tell," she said. "I can't go back to San Diego, that's a given. If I tap my bank account, it leaves a paper trail or cyber trail. Christ, I don't even know the terminology! I do know that they followed Johnny and me to Arizona when we hadn't even used a credit card for gas or the motel. Who keeps the hit men off my back while you're both off in Europe somewhere?"

Another time, the answer would have been immediate. He would have passed her off to Brognola or someone else from Stony Man, to place her in a safehouse, under guard. That wouldn't work today, for several reasons. First, the soldier couldn't call on Brognola or Stony Man for help. He had been pushing it, just asking Barbara Price for information on his target's whereabouts, and it had been like pulling teeth. If she was misdirecting him, the whole damned game could still be up for grabs.

Bolan's second problem still would have remained, even if Brognola had been cooperating fully on the mission. They had every reason to believe that agents of the CIA were linked, somehow, with the Valerik Family, and that meant any use of government facilities was hazardous, regardless of the separation between CIA and Justice. The American intelligence community was rife with jealousy, suspicion, double-dealing and one-upmanship. In Hoover's time, the FBI and CIA had barely been on speaking terms, each spying on the other when it got a chance, and while the old man had gone on to his reward more than a quarter-century before, old habits never really died. At least some agents of the Company were clearly operating in direct and flagrant violation of their charter, running some kind of domestic operation in the States, and it was probable that they had lines to Justice, maybe someone who would tip them when a certain female target checked into a safehouse.

Maybe Brognola.

Bolan hated to think so, but at the moment, virtually cut off as he was from Stony Man in every way that counted, he couldn't afford to rule it out. The big Fed had resisted and discouraged his involvement in the mission from day one, trying to sidetrack Bolan with vague allusions to some possible "security" involvement on the part of CIA. After his chat with Barbara Price, Bolan suspected Brognola had put a cap on any aid from Stony Man, although he couldn't ask directly. He had balked at putting Barbara on the spot, when it would serve no purpose. And besides, the telephone was a poor interrogation device. It always helped to judge the subject's body language, read her eyes.

He still hadn't responded to the question from Suzanne, and now he felt her watching him, ditto for Johnny, both of them waiting out his response.

"I don't like this," Bolan said at last, "but when you get down to it, I'm not sure who we can trust."

Suzanne smelled victory and broke into a dazzling smile. Bolan's announcement had the opposite effect on Johnny, though. His brother blinked twice, as the corners of his mouth dipped in a frown. It wasn't the decision to accept Suzanne as part of their road troupe that soured him, Bolan understood, but rather Bolan's confirmation that the three of them couldn't rely on Brognola or Stony Man.

"Okay—" Suzanne was bubbling "—I sincerely promise that I won't get in your way. Plant me in a hotel, and I swear to God I'll sit there in the room until I put down roots. But staying here...I mean, in the States—"

"Is not the best idea I've had all day," Bolan said, answering her smile with a twist of his lips that could have been interpreted as pleasure or a simple sign of resignation.

"So, Amsterdam," his brother said. "I don't know how they run security on baggage here, but I suspect we'll have to travel light."

"Affirmative," Bolan said. "We can ditch the MP-5s somewhere along the way, maybe a side trip to the river. Keep the side arms until we're in the terminal, then drop them off before we have to clear the gates."

From the expression on his brother's face, he knew he didn't have to spell out their problem. When they arrived in Amsterdam, for all intents and purposes, they would be unarmed until he could make connections with another hardware dealer and obtain replacements for their arsenal. If anyone was waiting for them at the other end, whether a delegation at the airport or a hit team on the street, they would be perfect targets.

Tolya Valerik didn't know they were pursuing him to Amsterdam, of course. The Russian should believe that he was running free and clear, unless somebody told him otherwise. And who would that be?

Maybe Brognola.

This time, he *did* go there, unable to deny the possibility, no matter how it might offend his sense of honor. Brognola—or someone in the loop at Stony Man—would be the only living link between the Executioner and Amsterdam. He hadn't mentioned going transatlantic, but Price knew him well enough by now to realize that he wouldn't allow Valerik to escape.

So, there it was. The simple act of finding out his target's European destination had placed Bolan, Johnny and Suzanne at mortal risk. It was his doing, and he had to think of something, quickly, that would mitigate the damage.

Reading his mind, Johnny inquired, "Suppose they're waiting for us at the other end?"

"What do you mean?" Suzanne was visibly distressed. "How could they be? I mean, how could they know?"

"I've got it covered," Bolan said. "At least, I hope I do."

"So," Johnny asked him, "what's the plan?"

"If they're expecting us," he said, "the watchers will be looking for two men, or possibly a threesome, traveling together. Our best chance to throw them off is splitting up."

Before Suzanne could protest, Bolan forged ahead. "The two of you will take one flight, I'll catch another. You can fly as man and wife, whatever. We'll hook up in Amsterdam and go from there. Play it by ear."

Suzanne's protest had turned into a smile of brief duration. "My passport," she began to say.

"We'll all need paper," Johnny noted, glancing at his brother. "Do you know somebody local who can handle it?"

"I'll find someone."

With the amount of cash they had on hand, most of it stolen from the Russian Mafia back in the States, he guessed they could have purchased diplomatic passports, maybe even royal ID, but Bolan didn't want to cause a stir upon arrival in the Netherlands. They should appear to be three common tourists, stand in line at immigration, smile their way through luggage searches if it came to that.

And improvise if there were shooters waiting for them at the airport.

Bolan had some experience with that scenario, though it had been a while. Returning from a French campaign, the first year of his private war against the Cosa Nostra, he had found a hit team staked out at the airport in New York. He had survived on guts and instinct, but his memories of that occasion made him anxious to avoid a not-so-instant replay. If the three of them were spotted on arrival, even if they weren't cut down on sight, they would have lost the critical advantage of surprise.

He liked the notion of Valerik winding down, relaxing at a brothel, maybe toking up some weed, imagining that he was home and dry. The Russian wouldn't let his guard down all the way, of course; no predator who planned on living ever did, but he wouldn't expect his unknown enemies to follow him across the sea.

Unless somebody blew the whistle.

Maybe Price. Maybe Brognola.

"Who's the artist?" Johnny asked him, shifting on the bed, a soldier anxious to be on the move. Beside him, Suzanne felt the energy and favored him with an appraising glance.

"The guy I'm thinking of sacks out until noon," Bolan replied. "We'll catch him when he opens up for business. Pay him double, and I expect we'll have our legends pretty well in shape by nightfall."

"Legends?" Suzanne asked.

"Our covers," Johnny told her. "It's a term they use at Langley for a fake ID with solid background."

"Ah."

"Who are we supposed to be?" she asked.

"Your call," Bolan said. "As a rule of thumb, you keep it simple. Nothing showy, nothing that you're likely to forget."

"So, I guess Meg Ryan's out?"

"No good," Johnny said. "That means I would have to be Tom Hanks."

Bolan was glad to see them in good spirits. It would help them face whatever disappointments might be waiting for them at the far end of their unexpected trip. There would be time enough to think about the risks while they were airborne, on arrival, while they stood in line at customs, when they went to fetch their rental car. Too much time, Bolan thought, but the anticipation—and the brooding—were as unavoidable as blisters on a long forced march.

So much to do before they left. Flight reservations were on hold, until they had the paperwork and plastic to support their reservations. When they dumped the hardware, they would have to take precautions, or have some trigger-happy kid or adult miscreant retrieve the guns and take it as a sign to blitz the nearest school or shopping mall. Their pistols, at the airport, would be easier. He planned to use one of those rented lockers, where you pay and keep the key. In most airports, security kept a close eye on the rented lockers, leery of bomb threats, automatically opening any that remained unattended for more than twenty-four hours. The pistols might cause a minor sensation, speculation on attempted terrorism in the media, but it would soon blow over when the guns couldn't be traced.

All right, then. They were good to go, just three more hours to wait, before their final preparations could begin. Bolan could feel anticipation building, like a tightness in his chest, and knew he needed to relax.

"If you two don't mind," he said, "I think I'll go back to my room and catch a nap before we start to make the rounds."

He left them there to talk or touch, whatever they felt like. The quiet, tender moments would be few and far between from that point on. He recognized the urge and wished them well.

He hoped both of them would manage to survive the days ahead.

4

The KLM Royal Dutch flight from Montreal's Dorval International Airport lifted off at 8:15 p.m. It was already Friday morning at their destination, though the sun wouldn't be up for several hours yet. As Johnny closed his eyes to rest, he pictured night-shift workers, janitors and such, going about their business in the darkened streets and alleyways of Amsterdam. It felt like looking through the wrong end of a telescope.

He needed sleep. There had been no time wasted snoozing after his brother left him alone in Suzanne's hotel room. They made love twice, the first time in a frenzy, slowing down the second time and willing it to last. Between and after, as they lay together, tangled in each other's limbs, they talked about the trip to Europe, what was likely to be waiting for them there. Details. They had tiptoed around the ''L'' word, shunning any mention of commitment as if it would be the kiss of death.

Their newly purchased passports had come through with flying colors. To the world at large, they had transformed into a married couple, James and Helen Blake, of Ottawa. The forger Bolan commissioned had suggested that the ''bride'' might keep her maiden name, a common practice with women these days, but Johnny was afraid two different surnames might have flagged them, just in case someone was checking airline schedules, immigration and the like, for

Johnny Gray and Suzanne King. This way, at least to an observer, they would be less likely to stand out.

Or, so he hoped.

If he was wrong, there could be hell to pay.

Johnny had been troubled by his brother's obvious misgivings, but relieved when Suzanne was allowed to come along. He told himself that physical attraction played no part in that relief, and knew full well that there would be no time for dalliance while they were working Amsterdam. If they had simply left her to her own devices in the States, however, Johnny was convinced that someone—from the Russian Mob, perhaps, or even Langley—would have tracked her down in record time and silenced her forever.

He would protect her to the best of his ability in Amsterdam, and sacrifice his life if that was what it took to—

"Are you asleep?" she whispered to him. Johnny felt the gentle pressure of her breast against his arm.

He cracked an eyelid, told her, "No, but I was working on it."

"Sorry." She retreated slightly, but his flesh clung to the memory of contact.

"That's okay," he said. "What's on your mind?"

She leaned back into him, as he had hoped she would, and kept her voice down. "I was thinking Mike looked kind of rattled, maybe I should say distracted, when he dropped us at the airport terminal."

Suzanne knew Johnny's brother by the name of "Mike Belasko," though he had another name picked out for Amsterdam, inscribed on a new passport, driver's license, credit cards. "That's just his planning face," Johnny replied. "He's got a few things on his mind right now."

"Okay. I hope you're right." She paused, then said, "I guess you've known him quite a while."

"We go way back," Johnny confirmed, but offered no details.

"You know," she said, "you kind of look alike, now that I think about it. Like you're cousins, maybe once removed. In fact— What's funny?"

He couldn't help smiling at her observation. His brother had undergone a hundred-thousand-dollar surgical makeover after the announcement of his death, some years ago. It was supposed to be a clean break from his old life, fighting solo with his back against the wall, a launching pad for his career with Stony Man. Ironically, the only things that changed had been his name, face, fingerprints. Bolan's life had come out of the brief detour and zeroed back on a collision course with mortal danger, stalking human predators. The only things that changed for him, in fact, had been his face and name.

"Nothing," he said in answer to her question. "I was just imagining a family resemblance."

"I suppose it's not so much the looks," Suzanne amended, "as the attitude." Her hand had come to rest on Johnny's thigh, transmitting warmth. "First time I saw you, I could tell that you meant business. After all the cops were finished playing mind games with me, I could see you took me seriously."

"Well, you had a serious concern," he said. "It didn't take a rocket scientist to work that out."

"It's more than that," she told him, as she gave his thigh a little squeeze, "and you know it. How many PI's would have stuck around with all the shi—I mean, the things we've been through?"

"I've developed what they call a special interest," Johnny said. He didn't have a lot of time to practice flirting, but he reassured himself that they were well beyond the stage of breaking ice. Also, his "special interest" in the mission wasn't limited to Suzanne's ample charms.

There was no need to tell her that, of course.

"It's really something, though," she said. "*You're* really something. Sticking with this thing when we both knew my brother must be dead, calling your friend to help, the things you've risked and done. And all that was before we started...well...you know.''

Johnny didn't regard himself as any kind of hero, though he had received more than his share of combat decorations while a member of the Army Rangers. It was one thing, taking chances—even taking lives—but what had they accomplished so far, really? They had bounced around the map and neutralized some of Valerik's underlings, cost him some money, but the man was still at large, and they still had no clue what he was planning with his cronies from the CIA.

"Sometimes," he said, "you see a job unfinished, and you know it's necessary to complete it. Not desirable or useful. Necessary. That was how it felt with you.''

"Regardless," Suzanne said, "I hope you don't mind if I put you on a pedestal.''

"Make it a small one," he replied. "I've got a thing for heights.''

"Too late," she told him, fingers moving higher on his leg. "It's big.''

The flight attendant passed them by without a downward glance. Johnny could feel the heat-rush in his loins, the color rising in his face. "Suzanne—''

Her fingernails were scratching lightly at his thigh, tracing the outline of his erection through faded denim. "Hmmm?''

"I'm thinking this isn't the time or place," he said.

"We may not have another time," she whispered, fingers still at work. "There may not be another place. Besides," she added, pink tongue flicking at the point behind his ear, "you'll like it.''

"Someone might come by and—''

As he spoke, the cabin lights went out in preparation for the in-flight movie. Here and there, a reader kept his overhead light burning, pallid islands in the dark.

"Alone at last.'' Her fingers found his zipper tab and

tugged it down. The soft, metallic purr seemed thunderously loud to Johnny, like a piece of canvas ripping.

"Hey, hold on!"

"I promise." Suiting words to action. "There's a blanket underneath your seat if you're the bashful type."

TOLYA VALERIK stiffened, shuddered, then relaxed into the yielding mattress of the king-sized bed. A muffled snort reminded him that he wasn't alone, and he untangled his clenched fingers from the auburn tresses of a naked girl who crouched beside him. She retreated with a sigh that might have signified contentment or relief. In any case, Valerik didn't care. The girl had served her purpose. He was finished with her now.

"Get out," he said. The girl began to speak in halting English, but he snapped his fingers once and pointed sternly toward the door.

Tolya Valerik hated to repeat himself.

His visit to the brothel had relaxed him somewhat, as sex always did, and knowing that he didn't have to pay gave him an extra kick, as if he were putting one over on the house. In point of fact, he owned the house, and half a dozen others like it in the city's teeming red-light district. Something like one-half of all the prostitutes employed in Amsterdam were Eastern European transplants, the majority of those employed or sold like furniture to local pimps by members of the Russian Mafia.

The new Moscow regime was A-OK, as far as Valerik was concerned. He liked his leaders weak and venal, preferably with kinky secrets they worked overtime to hide. Those whom he couldn't bribe or blackmail could be dealt with more directly, but he rarely had to take such steps. Most Russian politicians were intent on getting rich and fat, as expeditiously as possible.

They were a lot like the Americans, in that respect.

Valerik still had trouble understanding why Vassily Krestyanov was bent on spoiling it, returning to the bad old days when everything was underground, but it wasn't his place to ask. For one thing, he was being paid to go along, enough to let him retire in luxury, no money troubles for as long as he might live.

And, then again, he also had a sneaking hunch that Krestyanov would fail.

Valerik wouldn't say that to the former KGB man's face, of course. He wasn't suicidal, and he had no urge to find himself kicked off the gravy train. If things began to fall apart on Krestyanov, there should be time enough for him to jump before the train derailed.

Remembering the hell he had been through the past ten days, Valerik wondered if today, right now, could be that time. His only loyalty to Krestyanov was a peculiar blend of greed and fear, well known to those who make their way outside the law, in a milieu where the rewards were often great, the punishment for failure swift and usually fatal.

No, Valerik thought, it wasn't time to jump. Not yet.

He had sustained some damage in the States and Canada, but it was nothing that couldn't be fixed, once he eliminated those responsible for the attacks. And if he never found them…well, what of it? In a little while, it wouldn't matter, either way. He would be filthy rich, beyond his wildest dreams, and he could leave his "brothers" to their own devices, let them sink or swim.

So much for honor among thieves.

In fact, for all their talk of family and brotherhood, Valerik had never known a mobster—not in Russia, Europe, Asia or the United States—whose first and foremost loyalty didn't belong to Number One. It was the very reason they had chosen to pursue a life of crime, rather than attending university and scrabbling for a nine-to-five position in some blue-chip corporation.

Gangsters lived the way they wanted to, as long as they had money coming in and they weren't in jail, or hiding out from hired assassins. They could sleep all day and party all night long, or turn that schedule upside down, if they were so inclined. The top men had it all—including bull's-eyes painted on their backs.

Valerik had withdrawn to Amsterdam because he had a strong machine there, soldiers he could trust to kill or die for him, and fair proximity to other sanctuaries if the whole thing went to hell. Russia was home, though he preferred to leave it as a last resort. Worst-case scenario, he could retreat to Switzerland, maybe set up housekeeping in the basement vault of a certain bank, which he served as one of fourteen directors at large.

But for the moment, he was perfectly content in Amsterdam. His unknown enemies were several thousand miles away, while Valerik had his run of posh whorehouses, live-sex shows and "smoking" coffee shops that featured marijuana menus, all of it protected by police who specialized in keeping one eye shut and squinting with the other.

It wouldn't be a bad place to retire, Valerik thought, although he favored someplace tropical, perhaps an island where the palm trees swayed to ukelele music and swimsuits were optional on beaches made of sand as white and fine as processed sugar. Possibly an island of his very own.

Why not?

He could afford a small one now. And later on…

Valerik yanked the mental reins, rolled out of bed and padded toward the bathroom. While he ran the shower, waiting for the water to get hot, he studied his reflection in the mirror.

Still not bad, though he was creeping into middle age. The several scars that marked his body were a source of pride.

Valerik stepped into the shower and scrubbed the sweat and sex away until his flesh was pink and squeaky-clean. His mind was blank while he was in the shower, focused solely on the heat and suds, but stepping out again, he came back to the world of here and now. A world in which he still had work to do for Krestyanov, unknown assailants whom he lusted to identify and punish for their insults to his reputation.

All in time.

Before he concentrated on that problem, there was a certain item he had promised to obtain for Krestyanov. And he would be paid most handsomely, indeed. The item had already been secured, was safely stored in Russia, but its transport was a trifle problematic. He could never be too careful where such matters were concerned. Those who were hasty often wound up dead.

Or worse.

And there were much worse things than clean, straightforward death. Oh, yes. Valerik had dispensed enough death in his time, had seen enough friends cut down by the Reaper, that he understood what death was...and was not. He was experienced enough to know that there were circumstances that could make a strong man crave a blade across the throat, a bullet to the heart or brain.

Valerik spared no effort to avoid such situations for himself, though he might gleefully inflict them on his enemies. That was a major part of his mystique: a willingness to mete out pain and death beyond the wildest drunken fantasies of his competitors.

It was a point of pride.

Except, of course, when Valerik found himself on the receiving end.

He toweled off, left the bathroom naked, leaving damp tracks on the carpeting, and poured himself a double shot of vodka, neat. It wasn't good to drink alone, the Russian had read somewhere, but he dismissed it as the blather of some temperance fanatic, one of those who saw "addictions" everywhere. As far as that lot was concerned, someone couldn't eat, drink, gamble, smoke or screw without becoming "codependent."

Fuck them all, he thought, and drained his double shot, pouring another while the first was busy lighting fires inside him.

Come what may, Valerik knew his greatest pleasure, on his death bed, would be knowing that throughout his life, he'd made up the rules as he went along, forced others to comply, instead of bowing to another's whim. That didn't mean he was devoid of fear. Instead, he had learned to master weakness, make the best of situations where another would have cut and run.

Take Krestyanov, for instance. They despised each other—one a kind of rogue policeman, while the other was a smuggler, thief, assassin—but they both had dipped their hands in blood of lesser men. They shared a kind of minimal respect for each other, each content to use the other when it suited him.

Just now, Tolya Valerik was the tool, Vassily Krestyanov the draftsman, Noble Pruett his collaborator in America. Their tenuous association wouldn't last forever, though, and when those fragile bonds were severed, Valerik would be ready to defend himself—or go on the defensive—if required.

He had thought of double-crossing Krestyanov on more than one occasion. He hadn't abstained from any sense of loyalty or admiration; rather, he was set on getting paid for services rendered before he made any precipitous moves. Once he had *all* his promised money in the bank, once he had taken adequate precautions to protect himself, there should be time enough to think of making certain countermoves.

It might be wise, Valerik thought, to block Krestyanov's plan before it could be carried through to its apocalyptic climax. He could almost certainly have had the former KGB man jailed—and Pruett, too—by simply telephoning the authorities in their respective countries, after he was first approached to join their grim cabal. Valerik had connections with police in Russia and the States—God knew he paid enough of them to let him operate in peace—and they would be delighted to receive his information, make themselves look brilliant on TV. The little pigs who saved the world.

He hadn't called, so far, because there was a fortune to be made, and he could only claim the final payment if he made good on his portion of the deal. Once he had banked that cash, though, it would be a whole new game.

Or would it?

Krestyanov and Pruett both had friends, the skulking cloak-and-dagger types who dealt in black ops, wet work and subversion on a global scale. Some of them would undoubtedly survive a roundup, even if Valerik gave his contacts all the names and information he possessed. Revenge might not be swift, if he betrayed his partners, but it would be merciless.

All the more reason, then, for Valerik to pick up his payment and prepare his getaway before he contemplated any double cross. His action, if and when it came, had to take the others by complete surprise, take them down with minimal risk to himself.

And in the meantime he would have to watch his back. The faceless enemies who stalked him in America weren't the only men he had to fret about. If he was smart enough to think of double-crossing Krestyanov and Pruett, it was certain one or both of them had also thought of dumping him. The greatest danger would arise once he had made delivery on his promise, and before he had been paid.

That day was coming.

And those who lived to speak of it in retrospect would be survivors in the true sense of the term.

BOLAN WAS DOZING when the captain's disembodied voice announced their final descent toward Schipol Airport, eleven miles southwest of Amsterdam. His hair was rumpled in the back and the soldier combed it briskly with his fingers, reaching for the button that would bring his seat-back upright. He had flown first class and let Valerik pay his fare, with money stolen from the Russian Mob in California and New York.

The seat beside him had been empty, first-class prices being what they were, and Bolan had been spared the hours of tedious small talk with which some fliers felt obliged to torment strangers they would never see again. The downside of his solitude was that it gave him ample time to think, before sleep carried him away.

His brother and Suzanne should have been on the ground two hours earlier. Two rental cars had been reserved from different agencies, one for James Blake, the other Bolan's, in the name of Evan Green. He had avoided use of any pseudonym that might ring bells with Brognola or his compatriots—assuming they still were compatriots—at Stony Man. No Mike Belasko, nothing with his own initials as a giveaway. The Farm had ways of tracking travelers. Given sufficient time, Brognola could have made arrangements to review security videotapes from Dorval International in Montreal, but there was nothing he could do to guard himself on that end.

If the Farm was tracking him on Brognola's behalf, what would the next move be? He understood that Able Team was somewhere in Bolivia, while Phoenix Force was on a job in Southeast Asia, probably Bangkok. If either team had scrambled instantly, as soon as he got off the telephone with Barbara Price, they could be waiting on the ground in Amsterdam. In spite of the logistics, though, he was prepared to disregard that threat. The three members of Able Team were friends of Bolan, two of them bound to him by blood, before he ever met Brognola. All three wouldn't betray him under any circumstances, even to the point of giving up their lives, and the big Fed would know that going in. His ties to Phoenix Force were more recent, but no less compelling. He had fought beside them, risked his life for them, and they for him.

Who else was left?

Bolan was reasonably sure that Brognola wouldn't use Interpol. The force was relatively small, its agents chiefly watchers, rather than combatants. They collaborated with police in other countries, running international investigations, but they served no court system, maintained no SWAT teams, had no real authority as such, in any country where they operated.

Which brought Bolan back to Langley and the CIA.

The Company—or some of its agents—were connected to Valerik somehow. That much had been positively demonstrated in New York, when he had found a CIA man's corpse among the bodies of a dozen Russian *mafiosi,* at a warehouse where the fight went badly for his enemies. Bolan wasn't responsible for taking out the spook, but he had seen enough before the shooting started to convince himself that Langley and Valerik's Family had something in common.

As to what that something was, how deep the taint at Langley ran, Bolan was clueless.

But the CIA *could* set a trap for him in Amsterdam, if they were so inclined and knew that he was coming. Brognola could tip them off to his arrival with a phone call, or at least alert them to his likely presence in the neighborhood, if Stony Man hadn't nailed down his flight, and that could mean no end of trouble going in, before he had a chance to get his hands on any hardware.

Bolan had no problem squaring off against the Company if it came down to that. Its agents didn't fit his definition of police—particularly after rogues within the Agency had staged a raid on Stony Man, assassinating his lover April Rose—and they were therefore not exempt from Bolan's lethal wrath. It would be inconvenient, though, to fight a two-front war on unfamiliar turf, and if he had his druthers, Bolan would prefer to concentrate on taking down Valerik's Family.

For now, at least.

When he was finished with the Russians, if he lived that long, he would be very interested in nailing their connections in Virginia.

First things, first.

The plane was losing altitude, and Bolan heard the landing gear lock open with that thumping sound that always conjured mental images of road kill. Bolan scoped out the city rooftops as they were circling once around and back to Schipol. Seven minutes later they were on the ground and taxiing in toward the gate.

Schipol maintained its operations in a single terminal, arrivals on the ground floor, with departures from the floor above. Its user-friendly layout featured distinctive color-coding and multilingual signs telling the weary traveler exactly where to go. Somehow, despite a constant flow of foreign visitors, many of whom were drawn specifically by legalized commercial sex and lax drug laws, the airport remained one of the cleanest and most attractive in Europe— or in the world, for that matter.

As he entered the arrivals hall, Bolan kept an eye out for potential welcoming committees. Johnny and Suzanne weren't supposed to meet him at the gate, but someone else might very well be waiting for him. Theoretically, security precautions would prevent his enemies from bearing arms beyond a certain point, but by the time he breezed through immigration, claimed his bag and reached the signs directing him to auto rental agencies, he was in no-man's land.

The hell of it was that so many Dutchmen and their foreign visitors dressed up like spooks, which was to say, in normal, every-day civilian garb, nothing remarkable. There were no lurking heavies clad in black trench coats or dusters, none with the Gestapo look from Central Casting, nobody with telltale bulges to suggest a rocket launcher or machine gun stashed beneath his jacket.

This was how they got you, Bolan thought. As he prepared to chide himself for being paranoid, he flashed back to the mental image of a Russian mobster he had squeezed for information on his blitz through New York City. The old man, supposedly retired, had swung a mean umbrella, featuring a long, thin blade, painted with toxins that could stop your heart in seconds flat.

Watching potential adversaries for umbrellas now, as well as guns and cameras, he made his way to the exchange booth, dropping off a thousand U.S. dollars and accepting the equivalent in guilders. It didn't amount to much, but he still had half Valerik's stolen money in his suitcase, and he could exchange more anytime he wanted to.

Still no one tracking him, as far as he could see, when Bolan pocketed his cash and drifted toward the row of kiosks housing auto rental agencies. Avis had him covered with a four-door Volkswagen Passat, the stylish GLX. Only when Bolan had his keys in hand, when he was moving toward the parking lot where rental cars awaited drivers, did he start to look for Johnny and Suzanne.

The woman found him halfway there, appearing suddenly, as if from nowhere. Bolan marked a group of noisy Western businessmen approaching him, and as they passed, he felt an arm insinuate itself beneath his own. His first impulse was to drop his bags and slam a fist or elbow into the intruder's face but Bolan spent an extra heartbeat turning, checking out that face, before he caved it in.

Suzanne.

She beamed at him and fairly shouted, "Uncle Evan! It's so good to see you!"

While they were embracing, Bolan muttered, "*Uncle* Evan?"

"Johnny thought of that part," Suzanne whispered back before she broke the clench. "I don't think anybody's watching us, but just in case..."

She rose on tiptoe, brushed her lips against his cheek and left him with a memory of some exotic fragrance.

"Where's your husband?" Bolan asked, not bothering to raise his voice, though he remained in character. If they were being tracked by parabolic microphones or some such gear, their words would be recorded, whether they were whispering or shouting.

"He's around here somewhere," she replied. "He dropped me off to do the honors. You know how men are."

In this case, Bolan surely did. His brother would be cruising in their second vehicle, scouting the outside of the terminal for watchers, ambush parties, anything at all. It was a comfort, even though he realized the trap—if there was one—might be invisible until it was too late.

"We shouldn't keep him waiting," Bolan said. "I'm over this way."

"I'll go with you," Suzanne answered. "We'll meet him at this restaurant he has picked out. You're hungry, right?"

Bolan imagined Amsterdam, spread out before him like a feast, and said, "I'm starved."

Ironically, Amsterdam's red-light district surrounded a house of worship, the Oude Kirk—literally "Old Church"—which stood like an oasis of calm and spiritual reflection in the heart of a district devoted to animal pleasure. Cruising past the Gothic church in Johnny's rented Saab 9000, Bolan checked the passing sights, drinking them in.

There was a cannabis museum, devoted to a history of marijuana through the ages, and no end of "smoking coffee-houses," where tourists and locals alike could sample the latest crop. Throughout the district known to natives as *de Walletjes*—"the little walls"—prostitutes in various stages of undress occupied lighted windows a floor or two above street level. Pimps hung out around the brothel entrances like midway barkers at a carnival, adding their fervent exhortations to the lure of supple flesh displayed above. Between the brothels, theaters and cabarets flashed neon advertisements for assorted live sex shows.

"You don't see this every day," Johnny said, craning his neck to catch the scenery as they cruised along the avenue of skin. "It makes Las Vegas look like something from the Disney Channel."

"Dirty money, all the same," Bolan said.

There had always been a school of thought that said that legalizing vice—be it narcotics, prostitution, gambling or pornography—would instantly remove "the criminal element" from the equation, "clean up" the industry and grant the licensing government a vast new source of revenue, through taxes on the formerly illegally—and thus, unreported—business. In practice, though, as Bolan knew from personal experience, it seldom worked that way. When Nevada legalized gambling, its huge new casinos were built with Mob money, staffed by "gaming" experts who had learned their trade in bust-out joints across the country, and they robbed the state blind, skimming millions off the top before they ever got around to tabulating net income. Years later, when New Jersey followed Nevada's lead, the same men—or their sons and grandsons—opened branch offices in Atlantic City, to replace the underground gambling joints they had run there all along.

In terms of sex for sale, while Bolan was no prude, he recognized the same principle at work. Pimps still pocketed most of the money, while the girls or boys did all the work, took all the risks. Government control had made some strides in terms of public health, containment of disease, but it hadn't improved the lot of working prostitutes in any way that mattered. Even here, in Amsterdam, the Russian Mafia and other groups still dealt in what had once been termed "white slaves"—the flesh and blood commodity procured for sale by means that ranged from false promises to forcible abduction. Once the human livestock had been "broken in" with drugs and gang rape, it became a daily grind of degradation, while the cash poured into other pockets, other hands. From time to time, the media staged interviews with prostitutes who claimed to love "the life," but there was seldom any coverage of the darker side, the skull beneath the skin.

It would have spoiled the fun.

This night, the Bolan brothers had a change of pace in mind for Amsterdam's world-famous red-light district. They were on their way to strike a match and spread some cleansing fire.

Bolan's connection in the city had provided them with

hardware, in return for U.S. dollars stolen from the Russian Mafia. His stock wasn't extensive, but the quality was good. They had procured two Uzi submachine guns, one Galil assault rifle, and side arms—a familiar Beretta for Bolan, a Czech CZ-75 for Johnny and a smaller .380-caliber HK-4 autoloader for Suzanne, to keep her company at the hotel. With extra mags and ammunition, plus some Russian frag grenades, the lot had set them back nine thousand pilfered dollars.

Bolan meant to get his money's worth.

Their first stop was a hash bar south of Nieumarkt, where the grapevine said that harder drugs—cocaine and heroin, some crack and LSD—were also readily available to "special" customers. The ones who had sufficient cash on hand, that was, and who knew a simple password. For the address and the code, Bolan had paid a street snitch one thousand guilders, a bit more than five hundred dollars. For the same price, he had also picked up several other addresses and names.

The hunt was on.

"Must be the place," Johnny said, pointing out a corner shop ahead of them, to Bolan's left. The sign out front read Belladonna.

"So it is."

The place was crowded. Bolan made no effort to count heads, but it appeared that every seat was taken at the small, round tables, smokers packed into the booths on either wall. The atmosphere inside was hazy, like some cartoon of the classic smoke-filled room exemplifying dirty politics. He wondered if the "coffee" shop's employees wore some special breathing apparatus, or if staying high throughout each shift was simply viewed as a fringe benefit. He pictured giggling waiters navigating through the fog with mixed-up orders, bringing soup to someone who had ordered cocoa, bearing pastry to a smoker who craved pasta.

He would have to weigh the giggle factor when he made his move, allow for unpredictable reactions from the customers and staff. It was no part of Bolan's plan to harm civilians. The Executioner was after management, someone who had connections and could get a message to the boss.

"I'll go in through the back," he said. It would be easier that way, less risk to patrons in the shop.

"The alley, then," his brother suggested.

"Sounds right."

It was a tight fit for the Saab, garbage bins lined up, along with a pair of shady types lurking behind the sex club that was Belladonna's neighbor to the south. The men looked Bolan over as he stepped out of the car, and he was casual about the way he brushed his jacket open, showing them the Uzi slung beneath it on a shoulder strap. The tough guys turned and fled without a backward glance, no reason to believe that they were on their way to fetch police.

"You'd better circle," he told Johnny.

"Right." His brother had observed the confrontation in his rearview mirror, following the punks until they vanished into darkness at the far end of the alley.

Bolan waited for the Saab to pull away, then squared off with the club's back door. The knob turned in his hand—their first mistake—and the soldier took one last clean breath before he stepped into the toker's paradise.

It smelled like 1969 inside, and Bolan hadn't even reached the club's main room. With any luck, in fact, he wouldn't have to go that far.

The two doors on his right were marked with universal male and female symbols, advertising public toilets. One door on his left was fitted with a round window, reminding Bolan of a porthole on a ship. He risked a glance inside, saw two young women and an older man, all dressed in white, all busy stacking hash brownies and cookies onto plates, sliding more pans into the ovens.

Bolan left them to it, turning back to the fourth and last door. This one bore a plastic sign he couldn't read, which he assumed had to be some variation on the theme of Private or Employees Only. Listening, his head turned to one side, ear close against the panel, he heard male voices. It sounded like the men were speaking English, but he couldn't swear to it, as muffled as their voices were, competing with the racket of chatter and canned music from the busy shop.

Bolan tried the knob and caught his second break, went in behind a drawn Beretta, thumbing back the hammer with a sharp metallic click. Two of the four men in the room were on their feet; the other two were seated, one behind a teakwood desk that had seen better days. Lined up across the desktop were an even dozen clear plastic bags containing some white powder that was obviously neither talc nor Epsom salts. Figure a kilo to a bag, and Bolan was looking at a fortune, once cut and parceled out by grams for distribution on the street.

The two men standing both had buzz cuts, pink scalp showing through, one of them with a tattooed dragon coiled around his head, its long snout spewing flame above one eyebrow. The man nearest Bolan had dark hair, worn long and tied back in a ponytail. All three of them were younger than the guy behind the desk, a fifty-something man whose graying hair was parted on the left and combed across his balding head.

"You boys speak English?" Bolan asked of no one in particular.

"Of course," the man behind the desk replied. "I sense you are about to make a serious mistake."

"It wouldn't be the first time," Bolan said. "Somebody want to bag up the dope for me, or is this the part where you play hero?"

He had already determined that the three men not behind the desk all carried weapons underneath their jackets. When the moment came, all three went for their guns at once. The one with long hair lurched upward from his seat.

A slug from the Beretta met him halfway to his feet and slammed him back into the chair, his lips working silently while blood spilled from a neat hole in his throat. The other two tried to take advantage of their partner's death, catching their adversary in a cross fire, but it didn't work. Before the first man even knew that he was hit, Bolan was spinning toward his second mark, the tattooed man. He put a bullet in the dragon's mouth, kicking his target over in a lifeless sprawl.

The man behind the desk still hadn't moved, and Bolan passed him over as he swiveled toward the third gunner, marking his target by instinct. The shooter had a stainless-steel SIG-Sauer automatic in his hand. He triggered two quick shots before a Parabellum mangler caught him in the chest and pitched him back in the direction of a vinyl-covered sofa, sprawling half across it like a sloppy drunk. His two shots missed their mark, one coming close enough to hiss in Bolan's ear before they drilled the wall behind him.

Done.

He turned to face the man behind the desk again. "Now, do you want to bag that up," he said, "or shall we play another round?"

"I have a bag here, on the floor," the fat man said. His grammar was impeccable, the accent vague enough that Bolan couldn't tell if he was Dutch or Russian.

"No surprises," Bolan said. "Your life depends on it."

"I understand."

It took perhaps a minute for the plastic bags to disappear inside a leather satchel that reminded Bolan of a doctor's bag. He reached across the desk to claim it, wagging his Beretta in a signal for the fat man to stand. Reluctantly, he rose, hands dangling at his sides.

"I have a message for Valerik," Bolan stated. A flash of

recognition in the fat man's eyes was covered up a beat too late. "When he comes by to see you at the hospital, tell him this was a small down payment on account, for Billy King. Got that?"

"I don't—"

The bullet drilled his left kneecap, and his protest turned into a squeal of agony. The fat man flailed his arms as he went down, missing his chair and dropping out of sight behind the desk.

"Remember that," Bolan said to the empty space where the man had stood a heartbeat earlier. "For Billy King."

ILYA KRAPOTKIN didn't mind working the night shift when he was allowed to guard the stable. He was no great friend of animals, but, then again, this was no ordinary stable, and it held no ordinary livestock. It was actually a warehouse, where cargo was delivered, always after nightfall, always under heavy guard.

It was the cargo Krapotkin liked, though he wasn't allowed to touch.

The second week of every month, sometimes on Tuesday nights, sometimes on Thursday, women were delivered to the warehouse. There were never fewer than a dozen in a shipment, sometimes twice that many. The previous night—Krapotkin's night off—fifteen more had been delivered to the stable, fresh meat for the Amsterdam market.

Inside the warehouse there were stalls, much like an ordinary stable, with partitions made of plywood, bolted to the concrete floor. Each stall was the size of a small jail cell, with room enough for two cots and a cheap portable toilet. Since the women were kept naked, they required no closet space or clothes hangers—which would have been forbidden as potential weapons, anyway. There was an open shower area in the northwest corner of the warehouse, with drains in the floor, where the women were permitted to bathe twice a week, under guard. The rest of the time, from the moment they arrived until they were sedated and removed by those who purchased them, the captives lived inside their stalls, fed twice a day on stew or chowder, portions small enough that none of them would fatten up from inactivity.

Krapotkin wasn't supposed to touch the merchandise, and normally he followed orders, but there had been two or three occasions in the past twelve months when a particularly lovely prisoner had offered favors in return for some small luxury. A candy bar, perhaps. Some aspirin. A soft drink. On the rare occasions when he was unable to resist, Krapotkin always bargained wisely, and he always got his payment in advance. He took precautions there, as well—no teeth, no nimble fingers wrapped around the family jewels. He always had his chosen beauty back up to the bars that fronted every stall, bend down as if to grasp her ankles. He had one hand free to clutch her hips; his Uzi never left the other, just in case.

Most times, if he was satisfied, Krapotkin kept his word.

Unless the bitch seemed haughty, even in captivity, and needed to be taught a lesson.

As he made his rounds in semidarkness, more than half the ceiling lights extinguished after 10:00 p.m., Krapotkin made a point of checking out the new arrivals. Some of them were sleeping, physically exhausted from their trip across the continent to Amsterdam. Those who remained awake were silent. Still new to the game, they had already seen enough to know that any defiance would be punished swiftly and decisively.

The latest shipment came from someplace in the former Yugoslavia. Krapotkin didn't know if they were Serbs or Croats or Kosovars—who cared enough to keep up with the ever-changing labels in that war-torn region, anyway?—but he was reasonably certain they wouldn't be missed by anyone who mattered. The procurers were meticulous in that respect, eliminating any prospect of a serious complaint at the initial stage in the selection process. Asian girls were simply purchased from their families, while Europeans and Americans required a bit more work. The Baltic killing fields were happy hunting grounds, where disappearances were unremarkable and often unexplained. The Russian Mob had standing contracts with a number of the generals in charge of "ethnic cleansing," to procure the finer female specimens before they were diverted into labor camps or shot and shoveled into unmarked graves.

As for Americans, they were the trickiest of all, but there were ways to bag them, all the same. Right now, the FBI was searching for a supposed "serial killer" in Southern California, suspected in the death or disappearance of some thirty women. Only two victims had been recovered, both long dead, and the federal profilers would have been amazed to know that their killer was also deceased, shot twice in the head and buried in the desert, near Mojave. Only his legend survived, carefully nurtured by the hunters who abducted comely hitchhikers for sale as human chattel.

Krapotkin's secret wish was that he might be asked to join the hunt one day. He would be good at it, he knew, but it wasn't the kind of subject one brought up in conversation. Not with his boss at least.

How would he phrase it? *Ah, Vassily, I've been meaning to inquire—*

The shout cut through his reverie. It was a woman's voice, but he couldn't make out the words. Some Baltic gibberish perhaps.

"Over here!"

English, this time, and it was not the same voice. In fact, unless Krapotkin was very much mistaken, the second shout had come from a different part of the stable than the first.

What the hell?

It was unprecedented, yelling in the stable, much less in

the middle of the night. The last time he had heard one of the women raise her voice this way—the only time, in fact—it had turned out that she was suffering acute appendicitis. Surgery would normally have been required, but in the absence of a safe physician, she was strangled with a garrote instead, her body taken out to sea and dumped, with concrete blocks tied around the ankles.

"Help!"

Another voice, from yet another quarter of the stable. Krapotkin thumbed off the Uzi's safety and reached beneath his jacket for the compact two-way radio he wore clipped to his belt. There were two other guards—one in the office at the front and one on the roof, where he could scan the warehouse floor through any one of several skylights—and Krapotkin wanted both of them to back him up.

Neither one was answering.

Krapotkin felt a sudden chill, though it was warm inside the stable. One more failed attempt to reach his comrades, and he gave up on the radio, returned it to his belt. He started moving toward the spot where he believed the last shout had originated, though it would be difficult to say with any certainty. The warehouse-stable had been insulated so that no sounds could escape, but the interior was still one giant echo chamber, with the ceiling eighteen feet above Krapotkin's head. If all the captives should begin to shout at once, it would be chaos.

"Please, help!"

A third voice, he was certain of it—and a third direction, too. No sooner had the shout begun to echo through the warehouse than a fourth voice, and a fifth, were raised. The last one was distinctly Asian, and Krapotkin homed in on it, moving toward the three stalls in the southwest corner of the stable, where the five Korean specimens were caged.

He never made it.

Halfway there, jogging between two rows of stalls, Krapotkin heard a shuffling noise behind him, shoes on concrete, and he spun, expecting the other guards.

Instead he saw a tall man dressed in black from head to toe, aiming a pistol at Krapotkin's face.

The Russian was no trick shooter, but the Uzi was his trusted friend, and he had never missed a man-sized target at close range. He raised the SMG to fire, his finger tightening around the trigger...and the next thing Krapotkin knew, he was sprawled on his back, staring up at the skylights, pinned down by what felt like a crushing weight on his chest.

The man in black bent over him, went through his pockets and retrieved the key ring. Moving up beside the shooter was a second, younger man, also in black, who took the keys.

"We're short on time," the shooter said to his companion. "Let the first ones out unlock the rest."

When it was just the two of them again, the man in black addressed Krapotkin. "You speak English?"

The guard thought he nodded, but he wasn't sure. His head was gaining weight, somehow. It felt as if his skull had swollen to the bursting point.

"You're badly wounded," the shooter said. "I'll be calling the police and paramedics, but I don't know if they'll get to you in time. Your buddies didn't make it. If you live, I've got a message for your boss. You understand?"

This time instead of nodding his inflated head, Krapotkin blinked his eyes, the quadriplegic's semaphore.

"Okay," the man in black replied, as if Krapotkin had spoken. "If you see him, if your voice works, tell Valerik we did this for Billy King. You got that? Billy King."

Krapotkin blinked again to indicate his understanding, though the name meant nothing to him. Less than nothing. It appeared to satisfy the shooter, for he rose and stepped back, disappearing from Krapotkin's field of vision.

The Russian was aware of naked women passing by him, but for once, the fact of their proximity didn't arouse him.

Likewise, when a number of them paused to spit on him and curse him, the Russian felt no anger. He was simply numb.

Krapotkin held on, staring at the skylights far above his head, and waited for the distant sound of sirens that would be his only hope.

Billy King, he thought, and wondered if he should have recognized the name.

THE MAIN HANGOUT for Russian *mafiosi* in Amsterdam, according to Bolan's informant, was a "social club" in the Jordaan district, fronting one of Amsterdam's many canals, a block northwest of Greenpeace global headquarters. There was a kind of morbid irony in the arrangement, militant environmentalists residing so close to the place where mobsters met and plotted their narcotics distribution routes, the sale of human slaves, traffic in deadly weapons which, since the collapse of Mother Russia, had included military surplus nukes.

Riding with Johnny in the Saab 9000, Bolan tried to focus on their destination, but he still had trouble banishing the tableau of the warehouse slave pens from his mind. Through all the mayhem he had witnessed and participated in, for all the bloodshed, somehow he was still not jaded to the misery of innocents. The thought of what those women in the warehouse had to have suffered, what had been in store for them, turned Bolan's stomach. But it also lit a fire inside him, hardening his heart against the moment when he faced his enemies again.

"You think he'll make it?" Johnny asked.

"Who's that?"

"The Russian at the warehouse."

Bolan shrugged. "His boss will get the message, one way or another."

Johnny thought about that for another block before he asked, "So, what's the program when we're finished with Valerik?"

"Try to find out who he's working with," the Executioner replied. "Go home and mop it up."

"It never ends."

His brother wasn't asking this time, but he still deserved an answer. "No. It never does."

"I don't know how you keep it up."

"Clean living and the Golden Rule," Bolan said, startled by the smile that came, unbidden, to his face.

"The Golden Rule?"

"Do unto others," Bolan stated, "before they have a chance to do you."

"Sounds fair."

"It works for me."

The Russian social club was called Dzerzhinsky Square, after the long-time address of the KGB's headquarters in Moscow. Bolan supposed that it amused Valerik and his cronies to kill time at an establishment named for the agency once supposedly devoted to their destruction. On the flip side, though, bearing in mind the pervasive corruption of Soviet society, the deals often cut between hunters and hunted, he knew there might as easily have been another hidden meaning to the choice of names.

And at the moment, Bolan didn't give a damn.

They could have called the place Fort Knox, and it wouldn't have kept them safe.

"Looks like the place," his brother said, and Bolan double-checked the street address. A broad, tree-lined canal ran beside the two-lane street on Bolan's side, one of the many that had earned for Amsterdam the nickname "Venice of the North." He watched two couples pedaling along on a canal bike, giggling like children when a water taxi passed and left them bobbing in its choppy wake.

Tourists, he thought, and wondered what it would be like to travel with no purpose other than amusement, relaxation, fun and frolic. He recalled the brief vacations of his childhood, mostly spent at home, working through summer breaks from school once he was old enough. His first real traveling experience had come as an enlisted member of the Army Special Forces, and while Bolan's hellfire trail had wound its way around the planet, touching every continent, he had no photo albums, no home movies, no collection of decals. His travel memories weren't of galleries, museums and parks, but rather ambush sites, kill zones and smoking ruins.

"What's the plan?" Johnny asked, breaking into Bolan's morbid reverie.

The buildings, though of varied size and structure, stood together, no space in between them. None that he could see stood more than six or seven stories tall, those interspersed with one and two-story structures, giving the street an erratic, jagged appearance. All of the structures he could see—or their facades, at least—were built of brick and stone, as if their architects were frightened by the thought of fire. Dzerzhinsky Square was squat, two stories, flanked by taller buildings that precluded any simple access from adjoining roofs.

"Let's try the back," he said. "If I can get in there, you spot the front and make sure nobody gets out."

"Sounds like a winner," Johnny agreed, and took the next street to his left, then left again, creeping along a narrow alleyway behind the row of buildings.

"Here we go." The short club with its red-brick walls was unmistakable from either side.

"You want to try it while I wait?"

"No sweat," Bolan said. "I'll get in there, one way or another."

Johnny nodded. "See you on the street, then. Watch your six."

"You, too."

The club's back door was locked, of course. He had expected that. While Amsterdam could claim its share of

thieves, the upscale neighborhood and reputation of Dzerzhinsky Square itself combined to make this street one of the
safest in the city. Standard locks were all he had to beat, and
Bolan used his picks in preference to blasting through, and
thus surrendering the critical advantage of surprise.

Or, so he thought.

The lock was easy—twenty seconds, give or take—and he
was pocketing his picks, about to turn the knob, when someone on the inside did it for him. Bolan stood his ground,
confronted by a burly hardman six or seven inches taller than
himself, weighing perhaps 250 pounds.

The hardman's sneering challenge was in Russian. Bolan
answered with a straight-arm shot, his palm connecting with
his adversary's nose and splaying it across his face. The Russian staggered backward, grunting, giving Bolan time to wipe
his blood-slick hand against the wall and whip his Uzi from
underneath his trench coat.

Instead of firing, Bolan swung the Uzi's muzzle in a rising
arch, finding his adversary's crotch with crushing force. The
hulk expelled a kind of whistling squeal and doubled over,
catching Bolan's knee between the eyes. Another short chop
with the Uzi, this one to his temple, and he went down hard,
unconscious, maybe on his way to comatose.

Bolan took time to close the door behind him, stepped
across the sentry's huddled bulk, trailing the muffled sound
of voices to a steam room with condensation covering the
small, round window in the middle of the door. Beyond, a
few more yards along the hallway, he heard other voices,
riffling cards, the clink of ice in cocktail glasses.

Time to play.

The door produced a sucking sound as Bolan stepped into
the steam room. The soldier guessed the locker room and
showers had to have been across the hall, and he was thankful
that he wasn't wearing contact lenses, nothing but the steam

itself to cloud his view of towel-draped men, arrayed on benches lining three walls of the chamber.

Someone challenged him in Russian, and he let his Uzi do the talking, sweeping once around the room from left to right. Its stuttering report was thunderous inside the steam room, and his ears were ringing when he stepped back into the hallway, the familiar reek of cordite dampened by the steam.

A hush had fallen in the game room, up ahead, replaced by scraping sounds as chairs were shoved away from tables, soldiers scrambling for weapons in response to the sounds of battle. Bolan flicked a glance behind him, making sure the back-door hulk was still out of play, then he moved on to meet his enemies.

A glance showed Bolan that the troops were stag, no women to distract them from their gambling and vodka, no civilians to obstruct his line of fire. He pegged the head count at a dozen, give or take, but there was no time for precision as the room exploded into chaos.

To his left, behind the bar, a man almost as large as Bolan's late assailant in the corridor was cursing him in Russian, reaching for some kind of weapon underneath the bar. A short burst to the chest removed that threat and stilled his voice forever, as blood from ruptured lungs exploded from his mouth as he went down.

Bolan kept firing, saw a second Russian topple, and a third. Some of the others had their weapons now, incoming fire dotting the bar and wall behind him, spilling brick dust to the floor. He spied a shooter crouched behind a square card table, toppled as a shield, and stitched a line of holes across the tabletop. Bolan was rewarded with a scream and quick glimpse of the gunner's thrashing legs.

The Executioner took advantage of a lull to drop the Uzi's nearly empty magazine and slap a fresh one into place. Reaching inside his jacket, Bolan found a frag grenade and worked it free, released the safety pin and lobbed the bomb overhand, across the gaming room. One of his adversaries seemed to recognize the object lofting toward him, bolting from ground zero, but a quick 9 mm burst cut short his run for cover.

When the frag grenade went off, Bolan had time to glimpse a pair of bodies cartwheeling through space. Before they even hit the floor, a group of their compatriots were breaking for the exit, turning tail in an attempt to save themselves. He chased them with an Uzi burst to keep them moving, waited for a moment and smiled grimly at the sound of rapid fire from Johnny's weapon, firing from the street. Of five or six who had attempted to escape, one made it back into the gaming room, his white shirt stained with crimson from a shoulder wound, and Bolan dropped him where he stood.

A deathly silence settled on the killing floor, as Bolan rose from cover, moving cautiously among the dead and dying. There was no one he could count on to survive and bear a message to Valerik, but it didn't matter. If the Russian didn't recognize his own predicament by now, he never would.

And it was time to go.

Bolan was clear and moving out to the alley, heading toward the intersection, when a figure rose up from the shadow of a garbage bin on his left and stepped in front of him. He was about to let the Uzi handle it, before the figure raised its hands.

"Whoa, friend," the stranger said. "We need to have a talk."

"And why is that?" Bolan asked, conscious of the doomsday numbers falling in his mind.

"I wouldn't be surprised if I could help you with this job you're on."

"And you would be…?"

"Name's Able Deckard," the stranger said. He was smiling as he added, "CIA."

6

They drove around for fifteen minutes in a kind of numbing silence, while the Executioner decided what to do with Able Deckard. He had frisked the spook before they climbed into the Saab, surprising Johnny with the surplus rider as he slid into the shotgun seat. Deckard was carrying a 9 mm Glock pistol and a switchblade knife, both winding up with Bolan in the Saab's back seat.

"We ought to dump him now, right here," Johnny said, after they had driven several blocks, an aimless zigzag pattern through the night. His eyes were nervous in the rearview mirror.

"I was thinking," Bolan said, "that we should take him back to the hotel."

"You're kidding, right? He's one of *them!*"

"I'm really not," Deckard replied. "If I could have a minute to explain—"

"Besides," Johnny said, interrupting him, "you know the kind of shit they pull. He's probably got homers sewn into his clothes, inside a hollow tooth, some cloak-and-dagger crap like that. We take him back to the hotel, his buddies follow right along and box us in."

"If that's what troubles you," Deckard replied, "by all means, let me put your mind at ease." And then he rattled off the name of their hotel, the street address, the numbers of their rooms. Both rooms. "How's that?" he asked.

"All that tells me," Johnny said, "is that you could have your people waiting for us when we pull up to the curb."

"'Could have' is right," the spook acknowledged. "And I could have had some shooters waiting for the two of you outside Dzerzhinsky Square. I didn't, though, because I have a feeling we're on the same side."

Before Johnny could think of a reply to that one, Bolan said, "Let's take him back to the hotel."

"You trust this character?" his brother asked.

"Not even close," Bolan replied. "I'm banking on his brain, though."

"Say again?"

"I'm betting that he's not a stupid man," Bolan said. "I believe he's smart enough to know who stops the first round if we walk into a trap at the hotel. I also think he's smart enough to know we'll mail him back to Langley in a doggie bag if we find anything's been tampered with while we were out."

Thus far, no one had mentioned Suzanne King, but Johnny picked up on his brother's cue at once. "You got that right," he said.

"I mean," Bolan went on, "no matter what kind of artillery he throws around the place, there's no way both of us can miss at point-blank range. Okay?"

"I hear you, friend," Deckard replied.

"We're not friends yet," Bolan reminded him. "Just traveling companions, for the moment."

"Speaking of which," Deckard said, "we should really talk soon, before Tolya bails and you lose him again."

Bolan considered that for half a block, then spoke to Johnny in a voice that brooked no argument. "Let's take him back to the hotel."

Suzanne was startled and confused to see a stranger wedged between them as they entered, Johnny hanging back to check the hall outside and double lock the door. "Who's this?" she asked.

Deckard replied before the brothers had a chance to speak. "Miss King," he said, "I'm Able Deckard, from the CIA."

She stared at his extended hand, revulsion showing on her face, and took a backward step, to put more space between them. "CIA?" she said. "You bastards killed my brother."

"Which is not to say that I or my immediate superiors approve of what was done…or that we are prepared to let it pass." He glanced around the room. "If I could have a moment to explain?"

"I'd say it's time," Bolan agreed.

They all found seats, Suzanne and Johnny on the bed, a yard or so apart, Deckard and Bolan staking out the room's two chairs. Bolan had pulled his over toward the door, where he could pick up any sounds of footsteps passing by—or pausing—in the hall outside.

"You're following Valerik," Deckard said by way of introduction, "so I won't presume to tell you who or what he is. You've also picked up on a link between his Family and my crowd, but you're not sure what it is, how high it goes or who's involved. How am I doing, so far?"

"You're still breathing," Bolan said.

"Well, that's a start." The grin he flashed at Bolan might have been disarming under other circumstances. "What you don't know," he continued, "is the nature of the link between Valerik and the Company. You'd like to know who pulls the strings, and why."

"Still listening," Johnny said.

"Right. The bad news is, we still don't know who's working with Valerik, who employed Ted Williams—he was strictly freelance, by the way—or who killed Miss King's sibling. On the last point, I'm personally leaning toward the Russians."

"Is there any *good* news?" Bolan asked.

"Oh, I'd say so. For one thing, I found you before the Russians had a chance to take you out."

"That may not be good news for *you*," Johnny stated, "if the best you've got to offer us is double-talk."

"All right, then," Deckard said, "let's put them on the table, shall we? For some time now we've been aware that someone in the Company was moonlighting. It shows up in the little things—a piece of information gone astray, an operation that falls short of expectations."

"What you're saying," Bolan interrupted him, "is that you've got a mole."

"Not quite," Deckard replied. "The classic mole sells out and doubles for some other agency, most likely for another country. Aldrich Ames, the slimy bastard—sorry, ma'am— would be a case in point. This character we're looking for, or maybe more than one, is something else. At least, we think so, at the present time."

"Meaning?"

"Meaning that nothing we've uncovered yet points to a drain on critical intelligence, no obvious disinformation scams. The thinking is—and this is strictly off the record, by the way—that we may have a rogue or rogues inside the Company."

Bolan had no response to that. He knew what zealous rogues inside the government could do. They had come close to wiping out his friends at Stony Man not all that long ago.

The question came from Suzanne King. "Forgive me if I'm not quite up to speed on this," she said. "When you say 'rogues,' what do you mean, exactly?"

"More than likely it's an individual, or group, we can't rule out that possibility, who views himself in patriotic terms. You put him on the polygraph and ask him if he loves his country, loves the Agency, he'll pass with flying colors. Where he hits a snag, though, is believing that the system needs some kind of revolutionary change. Example—say you've got a cop who's been around for years, and he gets sick of seeing muggers, rapists, scum like that, go in and out the court's revolving door. One day, maybe he takes it on himself to do some vigilante work. He's still a cop, you understand, and he still *thinks* he's working for the law, but now he's got it turned around. Your basic rogue.''

"It doesn't track," Johnny said. "If you're right about this rogue, he should be trying to eliminate Valerik, not collaborating with him."

"Ah, well, there's the twist," Deckard said. "Bear in mind, the Company isn't a law-enforcement agency. We're set up to collect intelligence, conduct disruptive operations in the field from time to time, that kind of thing. We work with assets who, unfortunately, by the very nature of the business, you might say, are often shady characters. It's not our brief to bust drug dealers, or what have you. We're supposed to keep the country safe from foreign enemies."

"And how does that translate to working with the Russian Mafia?" Bolan asked.

"With the Russians," Deckard said, "it isn't always true that what you see is what you get. Tolya Valerik is a case in point. The man's a criminal, no doubt about it. He deals weapons, drugs, he's in the flesh trade—hell, you name it. If it's dirty, you can bet he's got at least one finger in the pie. And what that means, is that he's also got a list of contacts stretching from the States right back to Moscow. Contacts, I might add, that certain members of the Company would dearly love to make their own."

"You're saying he's a middleman in this?" Johnny asked.

"Very possibly."

"So, who's the other principal?"

"That's where the game gets interesting," the man from Langley said. "The Russian Mafia could never operate without cooperation from it's well-placed friends in government, you understand. Same thing as in the States, but they're more blatant with the payoffs, and the stakes are infinitely higher. While your average *mafioso* in New Jersey, say, is stealing M-16s from the National Guard and selling them in the Projects, scumbags like Valerik may be selling Russian nukes to charming fellows like Saddam Hussein. They've raised the ante off the charts.''

"And you keep track of deals like that?" Johnny asked.

"If we're on the ball," Deckard answered. "Which is to say, we try to catch more than we fumble. To be honest with you, we're not sure we ever got a full accounting of the Russian stockpiles to begin with, so it's pretty tough to round up strays. That's not our only interest in Valerik and his playmates, though."

"There's more?"

"You bet. A major part of staying solvent with the old regime was making special friends. The Russian Mob did favors for the KGB—procurement, wet work, low-tech sabotage—and in return, they got a measure of immunity."

"Sounds like our home team and the Bay of Pigs," Johnny remarked.

"You want to know the truth," Deckard said, "I suspect the Russians picked up better value for their dollars, or their rubles, as the case may be. Paranoia aside, we never had that kind of weight to throw around on the domestic front. With KGB, under the Soviet regime, it's like you had the FBI and CIA rolled up in one, responsible to no one but the President. They want you off the street, you're gone, regardless of the evidence. And, on the flip side, if they honored their commitments to a useful friend, you'd damn near have carte blanche."

"I take it that Valerik had some friends like that," Bolan said.

"Tolya had the best," Deckard replied. "Somehow, he got himself connected to a colonel with the KGB's black ops department, one Vassily Krestyanov. The Russians would have kept him on, most likely, after '91, but Krestyanov is a hard-liner. If the Reds aren't playing, he'll take his ball and go home, or into private practice, as the case may be.''

''The private practice being...?'' Johnny left the question dangling, watching Deckard's face as he considered it.

''You name it, Krestyanov will take a crack at it, assuming that the price is right. His specialty, under the old regime, was sabotage, subversion and assassination. All the social graces that supposedly went out of style with the cold war. He favors radical socialist clients, but he'll work for damn near anyone who pays his asking price—except the Brits and us, of course. When he bailed, he took a sidekick with him. Nikolai Lukasha, that would be, apparently a skilled assassin.''

''Why 'apparently'?'' Bolan asked.

''We could never really tie him to a hit, although we had reports from Russians coming over, this and that, claiming that he was good for twenty-five or thirty kills. That's a substantial body count for peacetime.'' Deckard hesitated, glancing back and forth from Bolan to his brother, adding, ''By our standards, anyway.''

''What's he doing with Valerik lately?'' Johnny asked.

''I wish I knew,'' Deckard said. ''Whatever it is, we've got someone from Langley involved, and that's got to hurt when it hits the fan. Unless, of course, we can close the show early.''

''We?'' There was no hiding the skepticism in Bolan's tone.

Deckard shrugged. ''Or not. It's up to you. Whether we play together nicely or agree to disagree, I've got a job to do.''

''And that would be...?''

''Sorry,'' the man from Langley said, ''I thought I made it clear. I don't go home again until I've nailed the rogues.''

THEY LEFT HIM in the room, chitchatting with Suzanne, and stepped into the hallway. Johnny wasn't thrilled about it, but he didn't let his paranoia run away with him. It was beyond the realm of plausibility that CIA had sent a man halfway around the world to infiltrate their ranks and menace Suzanne King. As for his real agenda, Johnny wasn't altogether sure.

"You buy that rap?" Johnny asked once they were alone.

"I'm looking for a trip wire," Bolan replied, "but I don't see one yet."

"You trust him, then?"

"I'm trusting less and less these days," Bolan said. Was that a hint of sadness in his voice? "There is one point in Deckard's favor. Once he found us, if he wanted us eliminated, he could've easily set us up. Have snipers waiting on the street, or something similar."

"How did he find us?" Johnny hadn't asked the question previously, though it had been weighing on his mind.

"My guess would be he's following Valerik, hoping he can find the Russians."

"But Valerik wasn't anywhere around the places we took out tonight," Johnny reminded him.

A shrug from Bolan. "So, Deckard followed him to Amsterdam, the same as we did. If he doesn't have a pair of eyes inside the Family, he'd have to go through the same process of elimination, more or less."

"Except he's not eliminating anybody," Johnny said.

"Again, my guess is that he was checking out the likely contact points when we blew into town and started rattling Valerik's cage. From there, you toss a coin. He either wound up at Dzerzhinsky Square by chance, or else he figured it would be a likely mark and staked it out."

"There's one more possibility," Johnny said, not elaborating on the theme. From the expression on Bolan's face, he knew he didn't have to spell it out.

"It doesn't scan like something Hal would do," the soldier

said. "If he was gunning for us, he'd send everything he had and try to catch us when our guard was down, make the tag without a lot of small talk. On the flip side, if he wanted to divert us on a snipe hunt, I'm inclined to think he'd send a friendly face, someone I'd be inclined to trust. Hal knows we're skittish of the Company. It makes no sense for him to send a spook."

"Reverse psychology?" But even as he posed the question, Johnny heard the clinker. "Never mind," he said before Bolan had a chance to answer. "Say this guy is CIA. In my book, that's the biggest reason *not* to trust him."

"Or, another way to look at it," Bolan said, "would be that Langley's cleaning house. They've spotted cobwebs, but they haven't found the spider yet."

"And Deckard's the exterminator?"

"Possibly. You know, the Company's been taking hits for thirty years, on everything from JFK and Vietnam to UFOs. Some of the things they've been accused of doing really were their fault, and others never made it to the media."

Bolan hesitated there, for just a beat, and Johnny saw the tightening of muscles at his jawline, knew he was remembering his former showdowns with the Company, the loss of April Rose.

"The bottom line," Bolan said, continuing, "is that they have a strong incentive to clean house. Ten years ago, there was discussion of defunding and disbandment in the Congress. If the spooks, even a few of them, were caught cooperating with a group of Russians in some operation damaging to U.S. interests, there'd be hell to pay."

"Which doesn't mean that Deckard's playing straight with us," Johnny put in.

"But if he is…"

"Two birds, one stone?"

"Without resources, he may be our only chance to reach

inside the Company and tag whoever's dealing with Valerik."

"You believe the rogue scenario?" Johnny asked.

"As opposed to thinking everyone at Langley, from the top down, is involved with Russians? Christ, I hope it's true. In the alternative scenario, we're screwed."

"You want to try him, then?"

"We may as well," Bolan said. "If I catch him doubling, I can always take him out."

It was settled, then. Deckard would have only one chance to prove himself. If he blew it, he was history.

Reentering the hotel room, it took all of a heartbeat for Johnny to note that Suzanne was in tears. He checked an impulse to charge Deckard head-on, instead asking, "What's going on?"

Suzanne sprang from the bed and ran into his arms. Her voice was muffled as she spoke, her face pressed against his chest. "My brother's dead."

She had presumably accepted that most likely of scenarios a week ago. Still holding her Johnny turned his face toward Deckard. "That's confirmed?"

The man from Langley nodded. "The remains were found three days ago, identified while you were airborne, yesterday. I got a call."

"So, you've been tracking Billy King, as well?" Bolan asked.

"Not even close," the spook replied. "I never heard of him before last week, when these two—" nodding toward Suzanne and Johnny "—got Valerik's people all riled up on the West Coast."

"Who killed him?" Johnny asked.

The man from Langley shrugged. "It could have been Ted Williams, maybe someone from Valerik's Family. The way it looks, from Ted's financial records, he'd been skimming on his handlers. Williams brought King into it. It's fifty-fifty both of them were ripping off the team, or maybe King got hit on general principle. Guilt by association, and all that.''

''In which case,'' Johnny said, ''there's yet another possibility. One of your so-called rogues could be responsible.''

''Same thing,'' Deckard said. ''They're all in the shit together—pardon, ma'am—and when they fall, they all go down.''

Johnny could feel Suzanne's hands clutching at his shirt, the fabric damp with tears. ''The sooner, the better,'' he said.

''I'm with you,'' Deckard stated. ''We partners now, or what?''

''Associates,'' Bolan said. And quickly added, ''There's a question that you haven't asked.''

''What's that?'' A smile on Deckard's face, all sunshine.

''Who we're working for.''

''Ah, well…I figure I know everything I need to know,'' Deckard replied. ''Miss King's been looking for her brother. Now she's found him, more or less. If all that grief's a put-on, for my benefit, then she's Meryl Streep, and I'm Mel Gibson. Which, in case your eyesight's bad, I'm obviously not. Miss King hired Mr. Gray, who's licensed as a PI in the state of California, to help her track down the brother.''

''That's two,'' Bolan said.

''As for yourself,'' Deckard said with a shrug, ''I don't need Sherlock Holmes to tell me you're a stone professional. Maybe you're private, maybe not. You're not from my shop, anyway. Beyond that point, I'm thinking that the less I know, the better chance we both stand of surviving this, without some stupid-ass *High Noon* scenario. You ever study Chairman Mao?''

Bolan provided the punch line. ''The enemy of my enemy is my friend.''

''Bingo.''

''So, what's the plan?'' Johnny asked, putting it to both of them at once.

"May I?" the man from Langley asked.

"Please do."

"You two have kicked Valerik's fanny up between his shoulder blades tonight, but he's still out there. I suggest you take a breather, while I tap my sources, maybe see what's rumbling on the grapevine. That is, if you don't have sources of your own you'd rather check?"

Bolan's poker face remained intact. "Why don't you check," he said, not giving anything away. "It couldn't hurt."

VASSILY KRESTYANOV, like any other bureaucrat, had learned to deal with setbacks, disappointments and surprises. That wasn't to say he was a patient man, that he enjoyed watching his best-laid plans unravel like a poorly knitted sweater, but he didn't panic, even in the most disturbing circumstances. It wasn't his nature. Those who knew him well had said on more than one occasion that when Krestyanov was faced with Death someday, he would attempt to con the bastard into giving him some extra time—and, failing that, that he would find a way to stab Death in the back.

Such was the former KGB man's hard-earned reputation, and it served him well this Saturday morning, with Tolya Valerik on the telephone, once more delivering bad news.

"So, they have followed you," Krestyanov said. "Your faceless ones."

Valerik wanted to deny it, he could tell, but lying would be perilous. "They mentioned Billy King again, as if I knew the bastard."

"The American." It came as no surprise to Krestyanov. Whoever these men were, who had begun to stalk Valerik, they were both persistent and professional. If they had followed him from America, it would explain why Pruett's searchers were returning empty-handed. "Is the woman with them?"

Valerik hesitated, then replied, "Who knows? My soldiers still can't find them."

"That's unfortunate," Krestyanov said. "Perhaps the next time they attack, you will have better luck. Meanwhile, I hope this sideshow won't distract you any further from your primary responsibility."

"I'll have the merchandise by Monday," Valerik answered. "Tuesday, at the very latest."

"I have your word on that," Krestyanov said, making it known that any failure to fulfill the solemn promise would have catastrophic consequences.

"You have my word," Valerik said. He sounded none too pleased about it, but his happiness was no concern of Krestyanov's.

"If I can be of any small assistance in this matter..." Emphasizing *small,* because he had no wish to get bogged down in Valerik's personal misfortune.

"Actually," Valerik said, too swiftly, snapping at the bait, "I wondered whether there's been any word from Pruett."

"Yes, and no," Krestyanov replied. "That is, we've spoken, but he has no information that would help resolve your problem. No one from his agency appears to be involved."

That much should have been readily apparent, even to a blind man. If the CIA had known of Pruett's involvement, they would certainly have reeled him in by now. They would be grunting him for details, if they captured him alive, and Krestyanov had no doubt for all his missionary zeal, the man would break. It might take drugs, or maybe some technique a bit more primitive, but short of death, Krestyanov knew that there was no such thing as holding out against prolonged interrogation.

He had participated in enough "debriefings" to be sure of that. Every man had his breaking point.

How close, he wondered, was Valerik to snapping, to becoming a danger to himself and those around him?

"I believe you should get out of Amsterdam," Krestyanov said. "Go to Berlin. Try to be circumspect, this time, and leave no trail."

"Berlin?" Valerik sounded apprehensive, maybe just confused.

"I will arrange a meeting for you there, with Nikolai," Krestyanov said. "Expect to hear from him once you have settled in."

"How will he find me?"

"You haven't been much good at hiding so far, Tolya. Nikolai will find you. Never fear."

It could have been a promise or a threat, Krestyanov realized, and smiled. Let Valerik sweat a little after all the problems he had caused. If his pathetic sideshow with the damned Americans endangered Krestyanov's grand *konspiratsia* any further, Valerik would do more than sweat.

He would bleed.

"I'll leave tonight."

"Why wait? Leave now, before your luck deserts you altogether and you wind up in the morgue. I have no use for corpses, Tolya."

Valerik didn't answer right away, and so Krestyanov prodded him. "We understand each other?"

"Yes. I'll leave as soon as possible."

"Perhaps a charter flight," Krestyanov said. "You'll have more privacy that way, and you won't be forced to wait on someone else's schedule."

"As you say." The proper tone of deference, but with resentment just below the surface, quavering, a tightly strung piano wire. A razor-edged garrote that could be looped around Valerik's throat with one phone call.

Krestyanov sensed that it was time for him to toss the other man a bone. "Be careful, Tolya. I wouldn't want to lose you." At this stage of the proceedings, he concluded silently.

"I'll do what must be done," Valerik said.

"I would expect no less."

Krestyanov eased the telephone handset into its cradle, watched the green light on the scrambler switch off automatically once the connection had been severed. Leaning back into the softness of his chair, the former KGB man wondered if Valerik, after all that he had gone through during recent days, was capable of carrying his weight, fulfilling his established obligations to the *konspiratsia*.

If not…

It might be wiser, safer, to eliminate Valerik now and start all over, try again with someone who wasn't embroiled in private, petty feuds. The loss of time and cash would be regrettable, of course, but Krestyanov had waited for the best part of a decade as it was, finessing details of his brainchild, the design that would restore him to his proper place, bring order to the planet once again. If he was forced to wait a few more months, the disappointment could be nearly balanced out with satisfaction from his punishment of Valerik.

No.

Vassily Krestyanov didn't want to wait if there was any way at all to carry out his plan as it had been conceived. Valerik had his problems, it was true, and Pruett had lost two men in related confrontations, but there was no reason to suppose their grand design had been exposed. Surely, if anyone in Washington or Moscow knew the details of the plot— even its broad outlines—there would have been arrests, perhaps eliminations, *something* to suggest the fact.

He didn't count the massacre of Valerik's soldiers, which appeared to be some kind of private matter, hinging on the death of an American ex-convict who, himself, had known no details of Krestyanov's plan. The dead man was a cipher, less than nothing in the global scheme of things. Losing a human pawn like that meant no more to the Russian than the death of an insect.

He saw now that he would be forced to kill Valerik once

the merchandise was safely in his hands. Krestyanov didn't mind. If anything, Valerik's death would be more economical than leaving him alive. Krestyanov would save cash *and* guarantee that Valerik never talked about what they had done together.

And the last part was especially important, since Krestyanov realized his *konspiratsia* could still go wrong. It was a minor risk, perhaps, but nonetheless a real one. If he failed, if one side or the other should react irrationally, without following the script, he might not save the world at all.

In fact, he might destroy it.

Still, it was a chance the Russian was prepared to take. The world that he had known from birth was already in shambles, ruined by a mob of idiots with good intentions. If he wasn't able to reverse the damage, heal the wounds, he might as well be satisfied to strike a match and light the fuse, stand back and watch the whole thing blow apart.

In which case, all his enemies would be destroyed, and there would be no one to blame him, even posthumously, for his acts.

It was, as Noble Pruett might have said, a "win-win" situation. Krestyanov could only hope that he would be alive to relish his achievement.

And, if not, his triumph would be written on the wind that scoured a blackened wasteland, perfectly devoid of human life.

7

The telephone rang twice at Stony Man Farm before the operator answered more than four thousand miles away. There was no salutation, nothing but a hint of breathing on the other end, no solid confirmation that the line was even functional. The farm's caller ID box had a lock on Bolan's number, though a trace back to the public telephone in Amsterdam would take some time. Meanwhile, if Bolan didn't properly identify himself within the span of thirty seconds, he would automatically be disconnected, nothing but a humming dial tone for his trouble.

"This is Striker," he informed the silent operator, "calling for Control."

"One moment, sir." It was a male voice on the line this day, which meant precisely nothing. With the hardware they possessed at Stony Man, an eighty-year-old farmer from Beijing could just as easily be made to sound like James Earl Jones.

Another forty seconds ticked away before Control came on the line. This time, he clearly recognized the voice as that of Barbara Price.

"Striker," she said, "are we secure?"

"My end's nailed down," he told her, glancing at the scrambler one more time, unnecessarily, for confirmation of the fact.

"Okay, we're five-by-five," she said. "What's up?"

"You stole my question," Bolan said, a shot at casual

levity that missed his mark by a country mile. "I don't suppose there's any further word about our mutual acquaintance over here?"

He was expecting the delay in her response, could almost see her frowning at his choice of words, rehearsing her response before she spoke. "No news on that front, I'm afraid," she said. "You're still in the same place?"

There was no point in lying to her when the trace would quickly show him up. Instead, he said, "I should be leaving soon. The way it looks, this territory's just about exhausted." Bolan gambled as he added, "I could use some leads if that's not too much trouble."

She was a bit too quick to answer, this time. "Where will you be going, Striker?" Recognizing her mistake, she added, "So that I know where to look for any information you might need."

"It's hard to say," Bolan replied, uncertain whether he was going anywhere at all, in fact. The action might play out right there in Amsterdam, or it might lead him to the far side of the globe. In either case, he didn't plan to telegraph his moves when he couldn't be certain of the loyalties at Stony Man.

"Well," she said, "if I don't know where you are..."

He tried a change-up, switching from his straight pitch to a curve ball. "How's our favorite uncle? Last time we talked, I had the feeling that he wasn't quite himself."

That stopped her cold for several seconds. He imagined Price frowning, concentration mixed up with displeasure, tugging down the corners of her luscious mouth. "I'm not quite sure I follow," she replied at last. "We spoke this morning, and he seemed all right to me."

Her tone said otherwise, but Bolan didn't feel like pushing it. There was nothing to gain by making her sweat, he decided. It was better to bail, before the conversation became any more stilted and uncomfortable than it already was.

"Okay," he said, "I'll let you go, then. Busy here. Places to go and people to do."

"You're taking care, I hope," she said. It was the first time she had sounded like herself.

"Hey, you know me."

"That's why I'm asking."

"Well…"

"Just watch your back, okay? It could get hairy over there."

"It's hairy now," he said. "We're sharpening our razors, though."

"Don't cut yourself."

"No sweat."

"Be careful."

He cradled the receiver, frowning as he stepped clear of the telephone kiosk. He checked the street for watchers, scanned the passing vehicles from force of habit, even knowing it was virtually impossible for anyone to recognize him in Amsterdam. That might not be the case, in fact, if he had been betrayed. If Brognola…

He didn't want to think about it, hated even having to consider the idea, but there was no way to avoid it now, after a second nervous conversation with Barbara Price. He didn't know if Stony Man had picked up any hard intelligence on Tolya Valerik's whereabouts or not, but he was sure of one thing: he had never heard Price so ill at ease before. They had been friends for years, and lovers on occasion, but her sudden reticence, her seeming inability to carry on a simple conversation, was entirely new.

And it didn't bode well for Bolan's mission, much less his longevity.

He had considered and dismissed the possibility that Price would betray him of her own volition. Even if he granted her ability to thus deceive him, she still received her marching orders from Brognola, and the problem had begun with the big Fed, a week before Bolan had placed his first call to the Farm, from Montreal.

And it was that fact that unsettled Bolan most of all.

If he had been required, one week ago, to short-list those whom he was confident would never turn their backs on him or sell him out, the first name after Johnny's would have been Brognola's, followed up by Barbara Price and his long-time comrades of Able Team and Phoenix Force. Now, almost overnight, it seemed that Brognola and Price both were lost to him, the Able and Phoenix warriors out of touch, somewhere beyond his reach.

But there was still the kid, his sole surviving kin. If necessary, they would do the last mile side by side and drop together at the finish line.

It never should have come to this, he thought, as he retreated toward his waiting GLX. The course of Bolan's life had been determined from the day he heard the news about his family, in Pittsfield, or perhaps his personal damnation dated from the moment when a homicide detective told him there would be no justice in a court of law for three lost lives. Like Old Blue Eyes, the Executioner had done it his way ever since, and while his various regrets in life weren't—like Sinatra's—too few to mention, there were none that truly haunted him. A man was called upon to choose his course in life, and once the choice was made, his other bridges burned, he simply had to live—or die—with it.

But Johnny…

There had been a time when Bolan honestly believed his brother would escape the cycle of destruction. After losing all his kin—three dead, the fourth a fugitive on the Most Wanted list. After the kidnapping by Boston mobsters that had nearly claimed his life, Johnny had been adopted by a loving couple, born again, in fact, complete with new, untraceable identity. He was untouchable.

But Johnny couldn't let it go.

His military service, which included decorations won in combat, had been followed by resettlement in San Diego, where he went to work, eventually as a PI. He had been drawn back into Bolan's world by a desire to help his brother, coupled with a yen for action and an inability to loiter on the sidelines when he witnessed an injustice.

Now, there was good chance that those very qualities, the things that made him who and what he was, would lead young Johnny to his death.

Too late to change it, Bolan thought, as he wheeled the VW into midmorning traffic, headed back to the hotel. Assuming he could pull rank on his brother, somehow, and prevail on Johnny to get out and take Suzanne with him, it would make no difference. The Russian Mob had IDed Johnny Gray before he ever reached out to his brother for assistance. They had tried to kill him once, in Arizona, prior to entering the fray, and there was no reason to think they would forget about him if he briefly dropped from sight.

And Russian mobsters weren't the only problem Johnny would be faced with if he tried to disappear. Brognola also knew that he was on the case, and while that would have been a comfort under other circumstances, at the moment, Bolan sadly viewed it as a threat. If the big Fed had truly turned against them, which Bolan was unable to imagine, then he couldn't afford to let the Bolan brothers walk away. In order to secure his own protection, both of them would have to die.

Slow down!

There was a world of difference, he realized, between the awkward reticence Brognola had displayed toward this assignment and betrayal leading to a murder plot. He was prepared to take whatever steps might be required to save his brother's life, but if the time came when he had to move on Brognola or his old friends at Stony Man, Bolan would only do so when the evidence condemned them all beyond the shadow of a doubt.

If he survived to see that happen, it would be the worst day of his life, but he would be prepared, and he would do what had to be done.

Brognola knew that, too.

And, one way or another, Bolan knew that time was running out. His game of hide-and-seek with Tolya Valerik had already spanned a hemisphere, and Bolan wondered how much longer it could last. How long before he pushed his luck too far, and it blew up in the soldier's face?

With any luck at all, it would be long enough.

For now, though, he had yet another pressing matter on his mind. He had, for all intents and purposes, joined forces with a member of the CIA, despite hard evidence that Bolan's latest enemy was also cozy with the Company. That was another source of danger to himself, his brother and Suzanne. Right now, in fact, it was more pressing than Brognola's machinations in the States.

Unless, of course, they were somehow connected.

That depressing thought perched on his shoulder like a raven hunting carrion, and rode with Bolan all the way to his hotel.

"Do you trust this guy?" Suzanne asked Johnny. They were in her room, both fully dressed, seated in chairs that faced each other, with the bed between them like a not-so-neutral zone. There was an Uzi submachine gun on the bed, where he could reach it with a minimum of effort, and a pistol on the nightstand, next to Suzanne's elbow. Johnny's CZ-75 was tucked into his waistband up against his spine.

"No," he said, "I don't. Not yet, at least. I'm not a great believer in coincidence, for one thing, and I've had some trouble with the CIA before this job came up."

He instantly regretted calling it a job, but Suzanne either

didn't notice, or she chose to let it pass. "Mike didn't trust him, I could tell," she said. "He thinks Deckard may set us up."

Assuming that was his name, Johnny thought. And he said, "It's possible. Whichever way it goes, he'll have to prove himself. Right now, I wouldn't let him stand behind me on a subway platform."

"So, why don't you just…get rid of him?"

The question seemed to stick in Suzanne's throat. Johnny had wondered, worried over how the violence might affect her psychologically, but thus far he had been too focused on protecting her from sudden death to ponder much about the aftershocks. Suzanne had led a fairly normal life before her young ex-convict brother disappeared. There had been Billy's troubles with the law, of course, but while his lifestyle troubled her, she hadn't wallowed in despair or misplaced guilt. Since hiring Johnny to investigate the disappearance, she had been stalked by soldiers from the Russian Mafia, had seen men killed and had killed a man herself.

Compared to all of that, the passion they had shared wasn't extraordinary. It could even be dismissed as a release of tension, a spontaneous reaction to the close proximity of sudden death. But Johnny wondered if there might be more to it than that.

Focus, the voice of his experience demanded. Focus and prioritize.

Mack was uneasy with the change in his relationship to Suzanne King, though he had kept his unsolicited opinions to himself. Johnny was smart enough to recognize the risk that he was taking, but he told himself that it would make no difference to his personal performance in the field. He was committed to protect Suzanne, and had been from the moment when she hired him to investigate her brother's disappearance. It made no difference now that they had been intimate.

"We're giving him a shot," he said in answer to her question. "If he's playing straight, his help could turn the game around. We know Valerik's operation is connected to the CIA. Deckard could be our eyes inside the Company if he's for real."

"And if he's not?" she pressed.

"We'll deal. There's always room for a remedial correction."

That was stretching it, he knew, until the truth ripped at the seams. If Deckard was a Judas and he found a way to set them up, they could be dead in seconds flat—a burst of sniper fire, a bomb wired up to the ignition of a car—with no time for a parting, payback shot. It was a gamble, three lives hanging in the balance, and while Johnny didn't trust the man from Langley any farther than he could have thrown a semitrailer, he had absolute abiding faith in his brother. If he saw fit to take the risk, then so would Johnny.

It sounded almost childish when he laid it out that way. He caught an echo from his too-brief childhood, heard his mother asking, *If your friends jumped off a cliff, would you jump, too?*

No way.

But his brother was different. He was a warrior and a born survivor. If Mack jumped off a cliff and beckoned Johnny after him, then yes, he'd take the leap. He might be scared blind as he fell, but he would follow where his brother led, and never mind the risk. They would survive or not, as it was meant to be, and if they didn't, he would go out knowing that he tried his best.

"I'm sorry," Suzanne said.

"For what?"

"All this," she said. "The whole damned thing. It's all my fault."

"You're wrong."

"Oh, really? Hey, the cops in San Diego knew my brother

was a waste. They wrote him off first thing, the way I should have when he started drifting in and out of jail. Now, all of us may die because of him. Because of me.''

"It's not about your brother anymore," he said. "It hasn't been since I found out the Russian Mob was part of it. Now, with the CIA involved for sure, and maybe remnants of the KGB, it's way beyond a missing-person case."

"And that's my point," Suzanne replied. "If I'd left well enough alone, instead of hiring you to help me look for Billy, none of us would even know these men existed, much less have them hunting us like animals."

"They haven't done much hunting lately," he reminded her. "I'd say we've got them on the run. And, just in case you skipped a page, I'm not your average private eye."

"I noticed that," she said, smiling despite herself. "But I've been trying not to mention it."

They were on shaky ground, he realized. With all Suzanne had seen, she still had no idea that Johnny and the man she knew as "Mike Belasko" were related, much less that she had been rubbing shoulders with the late, notorious Mack Bolan. She knew nothing of the operation Hal Brognola ran from Stony Man Farm—assuming that it still existed, in a form that Johnny would have recognized—and for her own protection, not to mention his brother's, Suzanne could never know.

"I'd rather not go into detail, but I met Mike in the service," Johnny said, surprised at how easily the lie took form. "We've kept in touch since then, and we collaborate on certain projects when one of us needs a helping hand."

"I knew it!" Suzanne blurted out. "You're some kind of a spy, right? Like James Bond or something."

"Nothing that official," Johnny said. "I'm an investigator, like my ad says in the Yellow Pages. What it doesn't say is that I also sometimes handle jobs beyond the usual domestic beefs and runaways. Sometimes it gets a little more… involved.''

"Like jetting off to Europe with machine guns and a damsel in distress," she said, no longer smiling. "Here, you've risked your life for me, and I'm not even sure if I can pay you for your time."

"You may recall we picked some cash up from Valerik's people, so I'm not exactly going broke. As for the other…"

He ran out of words, afraid that anything he said would either come out sounding cheap, some kind of loutish sexist crap, or else the kind of sticky sentiment you only found in romance novels.

"I didn't mean to put you on the spot," she said.

"You haven't," he assured her. "Not in any way."

"It's just not right, so many lives in danger over Billy when he can't be helped, regardless."

"Sue, I told you. This isn't about your brother anymore. I doubt he ever knew what he was getting into, and you're obviously not responsible."

"Then who is?"

"The men who put this play in motion, months or years ago," he said. "I'm still not clear on what they're planning, but it's international in scope. Your brother never saw the half of it."

"He stole some money from them, Deckard said."

"He said your brother *may* have stolen from them," he corrected her. "Assuming that he's right, I'm not sure that it really made a difference. With Russian gangs involved, a deal this big, whatever it turns out to be, it's not unheard-of for the hired help to be killed instead of getting paid. My guess, *if* Billy ripped them off, he only changed the execution date."

It came out sounding harsher than he meant it to, but Suzanne didn't flinch. Instead, she nodded, her eyes downcast, and when she met his gaze a moment later, Johnny thought he saw a flicker of relief behind her eyes. It could have been imagination, wishful thinking on his part, but at the moment, he would take what he could get. The last thing any of them needed was for Suzanne to become depressed and sink into some kind of guilty funk, where she got careless and reaction times began to lag.

"You're really something."

"Why?" he asked, surprised.

"I go to hire a private eye, and it turns out I've got some kind of James Bond with a minor in psychology."

"I hate to disappoint you," Johnny said, "but I look stupid in a tux, and when it comes to the psychology, I don't know Freud from Froot Loops."

"Uh-huh. You can't fool me. I bet you were some kind of whiz kid back in school."

"I'd rather not discuss my bathroom habits, if it's all the same to you."

That got an honest laugh from her, and Suzanne let it run its course. "You know," she said, when it was winding down, "I really don't mind being here at all. I'd rather be somewhere along the Riviera, granted, maybe soaking up some sun."

"Sounds nice."

"You know—" her voice had taken on a teasing note "—they let you sunbathe naked."

"I believe I read that somewhere."

"Do I shock you?"

"Nothing shocks me," Johnny said, returning Suzanne's smile.

"Well, then," she told him, rising from her chair and circling around the bed, "I guess I'll have to think of something new."

APPROACHING the hotel on a canal bike, Able Deckard scanned the sidewalk that ran level with his head, pleased that the great majority of passersby ignored him. Those who stopped to look were obviously tourists, with clothing rumpled from the suitcase, cameras dangling from their necks like bulky talismans. One dumpy looking woman paused to snap his picture, Deckard smiling up at her, then raising his hand to wave at the crucial moment, open hand blocking the camera's view of his face.

He had been working black ops in the field for nearly thirteen years, a seasoned veteran in anybody's book, and while he wasn't unaccustomed to the facts of death, this mission took the cake, in terms of body count.

Scratch that, he thought at once. Three years ago, he had been shipped off to Colombia, when narcoterrorists had blown up a commercial airliner, dropping 257 crispy critters from the clear blue sky. That had been different, though. For one thing, all the killing—well, most of the killing—had been done before he ever reached the scene, one tragic incident. This time around, it felt more like guerrilla warfare, and it showed no signs of slowing down. The very opposite, in fact, if he read "Evan Green" correctly.

That was one ass-kicking dude, by any name. Deckard would seldom bet against the house, particularly when the men in charge had access to the assets of the Russian Mafia, the former KGB and CIA, rolled into one, but there was something in Green's attitude, a kind of "screw-you-and-the-horse-you-rode-in-on" approach to life in general and warfare in particular, that made Deckard consider putting down a strong bet on the underdog.

Sometimes, he knew from personal experience, the underdog had teeth and claws.

Green would be needing every ounce of confidence and courage he possessed, thought Deckard, for the fight that lay ahead. Tolya Valerik wasn't beaten yet, by any means, and Green, with his companions, hadn't faced the Company, much less Vassily Krestyanov.

But it was coming. He could feel it, almost smell it on the

breeze, as he began to steer his paddle wheeler toward the bank. Throughout the heart of Amsterdam were situated moorings where canal bikes could be rented or returned, the one Deckard was making for an easy two-block stroll from Evan Green's hotel.

He had some news to share with his uneasy allies, after touching base with contacts at the metropolitan police and back at Langley. Deckard didn't know how Green and company would take the news, but he would lay it out and let them play it any way they liked. There was a chance they would bail, of course, but that was one bet Deckard wouldn't cover.

Not with Evan Green or Johnny Gray, for that matter.

He wondered, briefly, what their story was, how they had come to know each other. Separated by a dozen years or more in age, they seemed to understand each other on a level normally reserved for relatives or lifelong friends. Some kind of lead there, maybe, if he had the time to think it through. The Company had run a down-and-dirty background check on Johnny Gray, but it told Deckard nothing very useful. An apparent only child, adopted later than most kids—around fifteen—by what turned out to be a federal agent and his wife. He took the G-man's name, and it appeared no record of his birth name or his early background had survived.

Was *that* the key?

Unlikely, Deckard thought. Adoption records normally were sealed, and that wouldn't have been the first time that a file was lost or shredded by mistake, some clerk half in the bag by lunchtime, waiting out his twenty years, not really caring if he left a mess behind.

From high school, Johnny Gray had gone into the service—U.S. Army Rangers—and was decorated for his combat service in Grenada. Not the most impressive war to come along in recent years, but Gray had distinguished himself, rescuing half a dozen GIs under fire, smoking the best part of a Cuban platoon in the process.

So he was a fighter. That was hardly news after the rumble at Dzerzhinsky Square.

The kid had gone through college on the GI Bill, pre-law, but something changed his mind before he followed through. These days, he was a licensed PI out of San Diego, but that obviously wasn't all he did. Not by a long shot.

Evan Green, by contrast, was a total blank. To be more precise, the sweep had turned up thirty-five distinct and separate Evan Greens alive and kicking in the States. They ranged in age from thirteen months to eighty-seven years and change. One of them was a surgeon, and another one was on death row for killing homeless men with a machete. None of them, apparently, were waiting for him at this very moment at a hotel in the heart of Amsterdam.

The fact that Evan Green—his Evan Green—didn't exist told Deckard several things. First up, the guy had been some kind of soldier, once upon a time, but Deckard didn't have his fingerprints, and it would take forever, checking photographs against the files of military veterans spanning five, ten years or more. On top of that, there was an outside chance that he had done his service somewhere else, but Deckard hadn't picked up on the ghost of any foreign accent, and if they were forced to check the whole damned world, it was a truly hopeless case.

So, basically, he knew who Evan Green was not, which stopped a long way short of learning who he was. Some kind of badass soldier who had kept his attitude and honed his skills, while taking off the uniform.

Or had he?

For a moment, Deckard wondered if he might be dealing with a CIA "ghost." Distinct and separate from basic spooks, the ghosts were rumored to exist, but none had ever been reliably identified—at least, to Deckard's certain knowledge. Bottom line, the ghosts were said to be a handful of the best, or worst, depending on your point of view, recruits turned out by various elite corps such as the Green Berets, the Navy SEAL and Delta Force. They were so good, in fact, that Uncle Sam refused to let them go. He made the ghosts an offer they couldn't refuse: give up your life and be recorded KIA, slip on a new face and identity, then go on fighting, strictly off the record, when and where your country needed you the most. There were no resignations or retirements, so the legend went. You kept on fighting until you were really KIA, and ghosts who reached the big four-oh were rare enough to rank alongside Bigfoot and the Jersey Devil.

Ghost, my ass, Deckard thought, as he entered the hotel and crossed the lobby, waiting for the elevator, subtly checking out the patrons passing by. This guy was flesh and blood, with maybe just a touch of cold steel in the bargain. And the only thing that Deckard could rule out, with any certainty at all, was a connection to the Company. Green wasn't standard issue; he wasn't a contract agent; he wasn't a rogue. That much, at least, had been reported back to Deckard with an iron-clad guarantee.

And strangely, it had helped. Perhaps because he didn't know who could be trusted in the shop these days; maybe because he simply liked the thought of starting fresh.

Which brought him back to business, as he stepped out of the elevator, turned left down the corridor and started counting rooms. It seemed that he had barely knocked before the door swung open, Evan Green emerging to check the corridor in both directions, finally nodding him inside. The others were already waiting for him, Johnny Gray and Suzanne King together, side by side.

"So, what's the word?" Bolan asked him, as he double locked the door.

"Valerik's on the move again," Deckard said. "You can either let him go or follow."

"Follow where?" The question came from Johnny Gray, this time.

Time for the punch line, Deckard wondering how they would take it, as he said, "Berlin."

8

The gray Mercedes-Benz sedan kept pace with eastbound traffic on the broad Kurfürstendamm, which sliced through the heart of what was once called West Berlin. A dozen years ago, they would have had to stop within another mile or so, their progress interrupted by the Berlin Wall, barbed wire, land mines, machine guns.

None of that remained, but they would still be stopping short of where the wall once stood, a drab, inflexible metaphor of the cold war itself. How many men and women had died in the old days, trying to breach that barricade? How many had been killed since it came down in 1989, with all the ethnic and political unrest that rocked Berlin?

Who cared? Tolya Valerik thought, lighting a cigarette and gazing through a deeply tinted window at the traffic flowing past. Unlike Vassily Krestyanov and some of his old cronies from the Soviet regime, Valerik cared nothing for history, ignored politics beyond the bare minimum of knowledge required to run his business effectively, knowing which fat, venal bastards he should bribe.

Each time he visited Berlin, Valerik had the same uneasy feeling. It was nothing he could put a name to—certainly not fear, per se; more like a vague anxiety, as if he had experienced premonitory dreams of some impending tragedy, but couldn't recollect the details when he woke. It may have been the Nazi skinheads, their graffiti and the scars of violence that marked their passing, though he didn't fear them per-

sonally. As a foreigner—worse yet, a Russian—Valerik knew
he ranked among their mortal enemies, but he could pass
among them on the street, as pale as any of the self-styled
"Aryans," and they would never pick him out unless they
heard him speak.

"We're almost there, Tolya."

Bogdashka had insisted on driving Valerik himself, instead
of delegating the task to a soldier. Valerik sat in the back
seat. On the vacant seat to Bogdashka's right, a stubby
AKSU "bullet hose," dual 30-round magazines taped end-
to-end, lay concealed beneath an opened newspaper. Valerik
himself wore a pistol—the Heckler & Koch P-7, with its
squeeze-cocking mechanism—clipped to his belt, at the back.
It felt awkward, but its bulk reminded him that his business
here wasn't a social call.

He recognized the Tiergarten ahead. It was a park meant
for children, strollers, possibly for lovers, and Valerik felt a
bit like an intruder, though the feeling quickly passed. He
focused on the moment, on his purpose, and in seconds flat
was able to convince himself that he belonged there. He was
wealthy—within limits—and powerful—also, sadly, within
limits—and he didn't give a damn what any German peasants
thought of him, as long as they were smart enough to keep
their witless observations to themselves.

"No place to park," Bogdashka said. "I'll have to drive
around."

"So, drive." His tone was curt, his mind distracted as he
shifted in his seat, eyeing the portion of the Tiergarten that
he could see. Lukasha was supposed to meet him on the west
side of the park, near a wrought-iron gazebo where a small
brass band played polka music on the weekends. It was Sunday, but he hoped the band wouldn't be playing yet, as it
was still eleven minutes shy of 10:00 a.m.

"I mean you won't have cover," Bogdashka said.

"I have the pistol," Valerik said. "If it's not enough, I'd

probably be dead before you had a chance to help me, anyway.''

It came out sounding bold, but he wasn't expecting any danger here. Granted, his enemies had followed him from the United States to Canada, and on from there to Amsterdam, but Valerik saw no way for them to get ahead of him and set an ambush in Berlin. Not this soon.

Still, he was nervous as he stepped out of the car and waved off Bogdashka, watching the Benz merge into traffic, dwindling out of sight. His second in command would circle the park until Valerik returned to that spot, or until he ran out of petrol, whichever came first.

He faced the park and started walking, homing on the contact point. Valerik knew its general location, though he hadn't visited the park before. Within a minute, he spotted the gazebo, picking up his pace a bit, still without the appearance of haste. He was a bit surprised to see so many people in the park, this early on a Sunday, but he welcomed them as cover, simultaneously scanning each new face for a potential threat.

It had occurred to him that Krestyanov might try to rub him out, but he had finally dismissed the thought. Later, perhaps, the one-time KGB man might attempt it, but Valerik hadn't made delivery on their agreement yet, and if some evil should befall him, Krestyanov and Pruett wouldn't get their precious merchandise. Rather than start from scratch, with all the added risk, the fresh expenses, he believed Krestyanov would allow him to live a while longer.

And that, Valerik thought, could be the bastard's critical mistake.

He had no trouble spotting Nikolai Lukasha. Even dressed in casual attire, with sunglasses to hide his mismatched eyes—one blue, one green—Lukasha stood out in a crowd. At six foot nine, perhaps 180 pounds, he had the aspect of a walking skeleton, an anorexic zombie. The effect was amplified by sunken cheeks, thin lips and a receding chin below the hooked escarpment of his nose.

Lukasha never could have made it as a spy, since spies, by definition, were required to pass unnoticed as they operated on hostile turf. But he had served the KGB in other ways. A morbid sadist who could never get enough of death and suffering to satisfy himself, Lukasha was the leashed hyena who had followed Krestyanov on each step of his journey through the ranks at KGB, eliminating enemies and obstacles, securing such spectacular confessions, that it was said Krestyanov and his monster could persuade a stone to sing.

Krestyanov's resignation from the former KGB had been accepted with regret by some of his superiors, who realized the covert business of intelligence had to continue, despite the radical change in regimes. When Nikolai Lukasha left the service on the same day, following his master's lead, no one was sad to see him go. In fact, if he had stayed behind, without Krestyanov to protect him, it was certain that he would have met some fatal "accident" before the year was out.

Lukasha saw Valerik coming, flashed a mirthless, snaggle-toothed grimace of recognition before his long face relapsed into its normal cadaverous lines. As far as Valerik knew, that grimace was the closest Lukasha had ever come to smiling in his life.

"You're punctual, as always." It would have to pass for salutations. Lukasha didn't extend his hand.

"A small virtue," Valerik said.

"But an important one. Let's walk."

They moved together through the park, Valerik feeling almost childlike in Lukasha's shadow, though he was himself an inch or two above the average height for Russian males. Walking with giants clearly wouldn't serve to gratify one's ego. Walking with a psychopathic giant, he supposed, could be hazardous to one's health.

"You have misfortune," the giant said.

"I have enemies," Valerik stated, correcting him. "There is a difference."

"It is a hazard of your business, yes?"

"Sometimes. More commonly, I see it coming."

"You believe it may be something, someone, from beyond your normal sphere of operation?"

"If you want the truth—"

"Of course."

"—I don't know what to think," Valerik finished, as if Lukasha had never interrupted him.

"The colonel is concerned—"

"As well he might be." Valerik was pleased that he could beat the giant to the punch for once. It seemed to throw Lukasha off, making him frown and start again.

"The colonel is concerned that this unpleasantness may cause delay in your production of the merchandise."

"I don't *produce* the merchandise," Valerik told him. "I *procure* it from my sources in the military. If Krestyanov is worried—" he saw the giant flinch at mention of the colonel's name, as if it had the power to summon devils from thin air "—perhaps he should consult his own contacts within the army. I'm superfluous, it seems. A simple tool for Krestyanov to use without regard to any damage I may suffer in the process."

"There are reasons why the colonel may not use his contacts, as you say it. They are reasons that do not concern you. You've been paid most generously to *procure* the merchandise, and you should be aware that there are penalties if its delivery is interrupted or delayed."

Valerik flicked a glance at Lukasha and saw the sudden grimace split his face again at mention of the "penalties." He didn't need a roomful of psychiatrists to tell him that Lukasha loved his work, that it would please him greatly to mete out whatever punishment Krestyanov had decreed, should Valerik fail.

"What makes you think delivery will be delayed?"

"I do not think it," Lukasha replied. "I'm simply telling you. Remember your small virtue."

"I remember everything," Valerik said, and while he meant it to sound threatening, his own voice sounded thin and peevish to his ears.

Lukasha stopped dead in his tracks. At first, Valerik was afraid that he had pushed his luck too far, that Lukasha would grab him where he stood and wrap those giant hands around his neck. He wondered if the pistol tucked inside his belt would save him, if he would have time to reach it when the crucial moment came.

Instead of reaching for him, though, Lukasha checked his watch, some kind of chunky model with a thick black rubber strap, which still looked like a toy on the man's arm. Lukasha blinked twice, as if it was somehow difficult for him to read the time.

"You have five days," he said. "No more."

"My word is good."

"Do not allow this other business to distract you from your duty," Lukasha advised him. "Destroy these buzzing insects if you can. If not, ignore them long enough to see your duty done."

"Krestyanov won't be disappointed."

It was good to see the giant flinch again, reminding Valerik that he had at least one human weakness, but Lukasha swiftly recovered. "No one ever disappoints the colonel," he replied. "I see to that. By one means or another, he is always satisfied."

With that, Lukasha turned abruptly on his heel and made off toward the northern sector of the park with long, swift strides. In another moment, he was gone.

Valerik turned to the west and put the park behind him.

His brief confrontation with Lukasha left him out of sorts, and he could feel a headache pulsing behind one eye.

"Small virtues, yes," he muttered as he walked. "I will be punctual when it's time for them to pay."

THEY HAD DECIDED it would be best to drive from Amsterdam, three hundred miles and change along the high-speed autobahn, keeping the pedal to the metal all day long, stopping for food and gasoline as the need arose. Five hours on the highway, if they poked along at sixty miles per hour. Driving would also keep their arsenal intact and spare them from the need of shopping for new hardware when they got to Germany.

The risk, of course, was that they could be ambushed anywhere along the way if someone tipped off Valerik or his allies that they were coming.

Bolan took the gamble, and it was agreed that they would use three vehicles. He drove the VW Passat alone, while Suzanne rode with Johnny in the Saab and Deckard drove a Jaguar XJ6 sedan. Once they cleared Amsterdam, they made no effort to remain in contact on the highway, shunning the appearance of a convoy. It would be more difficult for Deckard to betray them, that way, if he was a ringer, and the odds against an ambush by Valerik's people, even without inside help, were likewise much reduced.

It was agreed that they would meet at 5:00 p.m., at a particular hotel on Friedrich Strasse, near the one-time site of Checkpoint Charlie, where Americans had guarded West Berlin and swapped spies with the Soviets for more than forty years. Before they reached that point, however, it was each man for himself, in terms of choosing routes and rest stops. If they encountered one another on the way, short of a life-or-death emergency, there was to be no sign of recognition, nothing to suggest that they were on a common errand with a common goal.

Bolan picked out the path of least resistance, passing through Dortumund, Hanover and Magdeburg before the last stretch to Berlin. He used the driving time to clear his head and sort out problems that had preyed upon his mind incessantly, from the Valerik-CIA connection and Brognola's strange aloofness, verging on hostility, to Able Deckard, the new wild card in the game.

Taking the last point first, he thought it would be nice to trust the man from Langley. Nice, but foolish, until Deckard proved himself with more than scraps of information they had yet to verify. He claimed Valerik had the jump on them again, a charter to Berlin, and Bolan gambled, taking him at his word. If it turned out to be a snipe hunt, then he would have lost a day, at least, and would be forced to look for other options.

After he had dealt with Deckard.

He had considered that the whole excursion to Berlin could be some kind of an elaborate prelude to annihilation. He had discussed it with his brother, privately, and decided it was best to forge ahead. They had no other leads, no prospect for assistance from Brognola or the crew at Stony Man, and there were times when anything felt better than stagnation.

The way they'd set it up, if it turned out to be a trap, at least they had a fighting chance of coming out all right. It would have been a different story flying into Tegel Airport, coming off the plane unarmed, the three of them lined up like targets in a shooting gallery, with nowhere to run and hide. This way, if Deckard had arranged a hot reception for them in Berlin, the hammer might not catch both brothers when it fell.

And Bolan meant to reach the Friedrich Strasse rendezvous ahead of Johnny, just in case. That way, if only one of them survived, he reckoned it would be the kid.

He had been tempted, driving on his own through brooding forests, skirting towns whenever possible, to find a public telephone and place another call to Barbara Price. Ironically, in spite of everything, it was as much an urge to simply hear her voice, as to collect new information on his moving targets. Even knowing it was nonsense, Bolan had a feeling that if he could talk to her one-on-one, however briefly, he could straighten out the whole damned mess, and so discover what had gone awry.

Strike three, at least while he was overseas. He couldn't trust the telephones at Stony Man, where calls could easily be intercepted, monitored, recorded, even traced.

That was the problem, Bolan realized. He didn't simply wish to speak with Price; he longed to see her, look into her eyes and read whatever truth was written there, for good or ill.

And that, he knew, would never fly.

He could no more present himself at Stony Man, things standing as they did between himself and Brognola, than he could part the blue Atlantic and jog back to Washington in time for brunch. The treatment Brognola—and Price, right; couldn't forget her—had accorded him since he signed on to help his brother with the job at hand, left Bolan doubtful as to whether he would even be admitted to the Farm.

Or having been admitted, whether he would be allowed to leave the place alive.

Forget about it.

He made a conscious effort to relax and focus solely on his target. If they found Tolya Valerik in Berlin, he hoped to have a conversation with the Russian *mafioso* before he ended it. Valerik might not want to chat, but Bolan could be most persuasive when he set his mind to it. He had a list of questions begging to be answered, and if he couldn't obtain the information that he needed from Valerik, Bolan knew that he would have to seek it elsewhere.

Possibly in Washington. Perhaps at Stony Man.

There was a great deal more at stake, he realized, than any simple scheme the Russian Mafia had thrown together for importing drugs, illegal weapons or undocumented aliens to the United States. The CIA wouldn't have been involved in small-time illegalities—unless, of course, the operation was designed as cover for some more important scheme. And with Brognola running interference for the heavies...

Bolan always ran up short against that same impenetrable wall. A few days earlier, he would have bet his life that Brognola was the straightest of arrows, the most honest man he'd ever known. He would have said that nothing could persuade the big Fed to betray his oath of office and the sense of duty that had driven him relentlessly since Bolan first laid eyes on him.

But something had changed.

The nature of his shift in personality, much less his motive, still remained unclear to Bolan, but he couldn't trust his life—much less his brother's, or Suzanne's—to Brognola, if there was any doubt at all remaining in his mind.

And so far, he had nothing else *but* doubt where Hal Brognola was concerned.

It was amazing, Bolan thought, how quickly trust could wither on the vine, simply dry up and blow away. He had been fortunate to find such trust at all, to hold on while it lasted, and he knew that it was pointless—almost childish— to preoccupy himself with feelings of betrayal when he had a war to fight.

A war to win.

Bolan wasn't conceding victory to his opponents yet, by any means. If they outnumbered him, if they suborned officials and seduced his closest friends, so be it. There was only one skill he had never mastered in his years of training and experience.

The Executioner had never learned to quit.

VASSILY KRESTYANOV experienced profound depression every time he visited Berlin. He missed the former "East" and "West" of it, the looming wall, the endless hunt for traitors, double agents and defectors that had been played out in that divided city for so many years.

What did they have today, in place of all that drama and intrigue, the endless struggle for predominance? The streets were overrun with foreigners, including Turks and Africans. The foreigners, in turn, were hunted by beer-swilling Nazi skinheads, who, for reasons best known to themselves, police appeared to tolerate, regardless of their crimes.

It was the same old fascist nightmare, born anew. Krestyanov was no prophet, but he had predicted what would happen once the severed halves of Germany were reunited, as they had been in the final days of 1991. The Huns had never gone for twenty years without declaring war on someone, pillaging their neighbors, and the Russian saw the warning signs on every side, as he killed time in the café, waiting for Nikolai Lukasha to return.

Aside from the official negligence in curbing fascist street gangs, there were aging Nazis and their unrepentant children staffing crucial agencies at every level of the German government. The laws against display of swastikas and other hate crimes were enforced unevenly, at best. New laws aimed at restricting immigration had a sharp, distinctive smell about them that harked back to Nuremburg.

Vassily Krestyanov, for his part, wasn't shocked by these developments. In fact, he welcomed them. It served his purpose for the widely advertised "New Germany" to drop its mask and show the world at large a grinning fascist death's-head underneath. Krestyanov blessed the Huns for being so predictable, thus sparing him another tiresome chore.

If they hadn't spawned neo-Nazis on their own, Krestyanov would've had to do the job himself.

It was essential to his global chess game that the pieces should be in their proper places, ready for him, when he made his final move. There had to be fear at home, while righteous anger seethed in the United States. While Noble Pruett dealt with his alleged superiors in Washington, Krestyanov and his allies would be hard at work in Moscow, painting over the bizarre graffiti of a mighty nation that had briefly lost its way. And when his job was done...

Checkmate!

But first, he needed iron-clad reassurance from Valerik that his merchandise would be delivered as promised, intact and on time.

He was about to flag down the waiter and ask for vodka when he realized that it was barely half-past ten o'clock, and he had chosen a café that seemed to have no liquor license. Quietly amused that he had managed to outwit himself, Krestyanov sipped his coffee, doggedly resisting an urge to check the time again.

Lukasha wasn't tardy yet, and he would have to make allowances, in any case. Valerik may have dragged out the meeting, whining about his problems, the attempts made on his life. Krestyanov was disturbed by those developments, of course, but he did not intend to let them spoil his day, much less sidetrack his master plan. What mattered, first and foremost, was Valerik's promise that the merchandise would be available on time.

If it wasn't...

Krestyanov was considering a range of suitable, excruciating punishments when he saw Lukasha approaching from the north, his head and shoulders visible above the hats and hairdos of his fellow strollers. The sunglasses he wore made his long face seem even more brutish than it was.

Poor Nikolai.

The giant had grown up with only one ambition, coveting the lifestyle he imagined had to belong to spies. Cruel Nature had enjoyed a joke at his expense, however, causing him to grow a full foot taller than his father, making him a curiosity

to normal human beings. Krestyanov could no more send
Lukasha on a secret mission than he could the tattooed man
or bearded lady from a circus.

Still, the giant had his uses.

For one thing, he was absolutely fearless, sometimes to the
point of being foolhardy. Lukasha's psychological evalua-
tions chalked up his icy courage to lack of imagination, coupled with a death wish, nursed subconsciously from adolescence, when his size made him the butt of jokes in school.
Lukasha was a sadist, too, and thus perpetually useful in
Krestyanov's line of work. The latter trait, according to the
analysts who'd studied him, derived in roughly equal parts
from childhood molestation and a craving for revenge against
the peers who had reviled him.

Krestyanov understood what the head-doctors had reported
and dismissed most of it as irrelevant. The only thing that
mattered in his world was Lukasha's brute savagery, and
Krestyanov's ability to channel it, control the giant as he
would a trained attack dog.

So far, Lukasha had never let him down.

Krestyanov paid his bill and left the restaurant before Lukasha had a chance to cross the street and join him. Lukasha
would never pass for inconspicuous, but if they had to be
seen together, Krestyanov preferred that it be walking down
a busy street, rather than seated in a small café where every
eye—and ear—was focused on the giant.

Lukasha was waiting for the traffic light to change, allow-
ing him to cross the street, when he saw Krestyanov, picked
up the signal to advance no farther and stepped back to wait.
Krestyanov walked past him at the intersection, slowing
enough for Lukasha to catch up with him in the middle of
the block.

"How is our worried friend?" he asked.

"Still nervous," Lukasha replied. The giant walked with
eyes downcast, watching his feet. It was a challenge, with

those long legs, not to outpace Krestyanov and leave him far behind.

"He has good reason to be nervous," the former colonel said. "I'd be nervous in his place."

"I wouldn't," Lukasha answered. He wasn't bragging, simply stating facts.

"We can't all have your courage, Nikolai." Or your psychosis, Krestyanov amended silently. "Does he have the merchandise?"

"He says delivery will be on time."

"And do you trust him, Nikolai?"

The giant thought about that, covering a long half block before he said, "I trust his fear."

It was a good, insightful answer, but it left Krestyanov wanting more. "Perhaps he has more fear than he can handle. Is it possible he fears these others more than he fears us?"

Another pause, while Lukasha considered this new riddle. Finally, he shook his head. "Not yet, but it may come to that. It would be useful if the other threat could be eliminated."

"I agree," Krestyanov said. "No word from Amsterdam, on that account?"

"Nothing. Perhaps they've given up."

Krestyanov didn't think so. Men who tracked Valerik from Los Angeles to New York City, from there to Montreal and Amsterdam, weren't the kind to suddenly get bored and drop the chase—not when they were on a winning streak, claiming one victory after another.

"We should prepare to meet them just in case," Krestyanov said. "They may be here already, feeling out the ground."

"What would you have me do?" Lukasha asked.

"Call Berghoff and request assistance. He has soldiers and connections to the counterterrorist police. What are they called again?"

"GSG-9," Lukasha said.

"Of course." Krestyanov was familiar with Grenzschutz-gruppe-9—most intimately so, in fact—but there were times when it pleased him to toss the giant a bone, make the giant feel like his equal, even slightly superior on some minor point. It kept Lukasha happy, and it cost Krestyanov nothing.

"You want the commandos, then?"

"Not yet, but they should be prepared," the former colonel answered. "It will serve our interest to see this matter settled. We have wasted too much time already. Let them end it here, on neutral ground."

"It shall be done." That quiet confidence again, refusing to admit the prospect of defeat. Krestyanov wondered, not for the first time, if the giant truly possessed that much faith in himself, or if, at some level, he was a hopeless idiot.

"As for the merchandise," Krestyanov said, "make sure our men are ready, waiting at the rendezvous. I want them there a day ahead of time, and no excuses."

"Done."

Krestyanov willed a smile to lift the corners of his narrow mouth. "You never fail me, Nikolai," he said, amazed to see the giant blush. "When this is finished and we have restored the motherland to the position she deserves, we must consider your promotion. Would you like to run the KGB?"

Lukasha grimaced, flashing crooked yellow fangs. A heart-felt smile, of sorts.

"You are too generous," he said.

"Who more deserving than yourself of some reward?" Krestyanov asked.

The giant, speechless, raised a massive hand and reached behind the dark lens of his sunglasses, dabbing moist eyes with an index finger the size of a fat cigar.

"Too generous," he said again, his voice cracking.

God preserve me from the lunatics, Krestyanov thought. But not just yet.

9

The rendezvous on Friedrich Strasse went like clockwork, with Johnny having dropped off Suzanne at a small hotel unknown to Deckard, prior to meeting his brother and the CIA man, as agreed. She had her automatic pistol and a suitcase filled with money just in case he didn't make it back, a fail-safe system worked out by the brothers prior to leaving Amsterdam.

Deckard had smiled and nodded at the small deception. "That's good thinking," he congratulated them. "No reason you should trust me yet—although, I must say you've gone way out on a limb, this trip and all."

"You're out there with us," Bolan had reminded him. "And I'm holding the chain saw."

"Fair enough," the man from Langley said. "Now, shall we get to work, or what?"

Bolan had rolled the dice by simply coming to Berlin on Deckard's say-so, and he rolled again, letting the spook select their targets for a quick sweep, just to let the heavies know they were in town. Assuming that Valerik had arrived ahead of them, as Deckard claimed, new evidence of being stalked across the continent could only drive him closer to the edge.

And when he got there, Bolan would be waiting to deliver one last shove.

"Valerik's got a place on the canal, Bruck Strasse, where his people cut drugs and package it for resale on the street. He's always got a stash there, waiting to move through."

"Suits me," Bolan said, looking at Johnny, who responded with a nod.

They took two cars, Johnny driving the Saab, while Bolan rode shotgun in the Jaguar. He didn't ask how Deckard could afford the luxury sedan, assuming that the Company was picking up the tab. Your tax dollars at work, he reflected, and couldn't remember when he last had filed a tax return.

Deckard drove like a man who knew his way around Berlin, and Bolan left him to it, ticking the street names off against a road map he had studied back on Friedrich Strasse while he waited for the others to arrive. At the same time, he kept his eyes peeled for a tail of any kind, checking the mirror on his side, alert for any vehicles that followed them through one too many turns.

They came up clean, as far as he could tell. Even Johnny's Saab was invisible. They traveled for three-quarters of a mile, passing a shop and an apartment block that bore the marks of firebombs thrown in riots, before Deckard's voice cut through his reverie.

"Looks like the place," he said, and Bolan raised his eyes in time to see the Saab just approaching. Johnny had boxed the block and come around to meet them, watching out for any indications of an ambush as he drove.

The Saab rolled past and Johnny flashed a thumbs-up, driving on to the next intersection where he turned left, out of sight, and disappeared. Deckard found a parking space across the street and backed the Jaguar into it, ready to clear the scene in haste if it was called for. By the time he switched off the engine and set the parking brake, Johnny was walking toward them through a drizzling rain, his broad shoulders hunched inside the trench coat that concealed his hardware.

Deckard held the briefing while they were standing in a huddle, underneath the awning of a bakery across the street from their intended target. "What we've got," he told the brothers, "is your basic cutting plant, so maybe you'll need these."

He fished around inside a pocket of his raincoat and came out with a couple of surgical masks, passing them to Bolan and Johnny. "I don't want you getting high on anything but pure adrenaline," he told them, smiling.

"Where'd you get the intel on this place?" Johnny inquired.

"Friend of a friend," Deckard said. "You know how it goes."

That could mean anything from DEA to an informant in the Russian Mob itself. There seemed to be no point in grilling him, and Bolan let it go. "So, what's the layout?"

"That's a dress shop on the street," Deckard replied. "The next three floors are residential. Our gig's on the top, accessed by the fire escape and service elevator, both around in back."

"Security?" Johnny asked.

"Bound to be," the man from Langley said, "but I don't have the details. Figure two, three shooters, minimum. They may have cameras, but I couldn't prove it."

"So, we go in blind."

"The main thing's going in," Deckard replied.

"I like to plan on getting out, whenever possible."

"We're wasting time," Bolan said. "Deckard, you and I can take the elevator. We'll give Johnny five to make the fire escape and find a way in from the roof."

"Suits me." The spook seemed perfectly at ease, as if he had no interest in specific points of strategy. Was that self-confidence, or did it mean the place was so well covered that they didn't stand a chance of getting out alive?

"Let's do it," Johnny said, leading the way across the street and into an alley lined with tidy trash cans, none of them conspicuously dinged or damaged. Were the natives all this tidy, Bolan wondered, or did vandals simply shy away from any contact with the Russian Mafia?

The fire escape was well-oiled, nearly silent, as they hooked the bottom section down and Bolan held it for his brother. Johnny hauled it up behind him once he gained the first platform, then drew his Uzi from beneath the trench coat, climbing rapidly, checking the windows as he passed until he reached the roof and disappeared once more.

"Our turn," Deckard stated, opening the back door, which was unlocked, waiting for them. "After you."

"It's no time for courtesy," the Executioner replied. "You know the way. Lead on."

Deckard complied without an argument, and Bolan followed him along a murky hallway to the service elevator. It was standing empty, with the doors wide open.

Too fortuitous?

They stepped inside together, Bolan with his right hand locked around the Uzi's pistol grip, his index finger on the trigger, safety off. Whatever happened in the next few moments, if he had the slightest reason to believe Deckard had sold him out, the spook was dead. It didn't matter if the second shot of the engagement cut him down; his first would send the man from Langley straight to hell.

It should have been a short ride, up to four, but Bolan's apprehension and the ancient elevator's creaky mechanism made it seem to last an hour. Passing three, Deckard slipped on his paper mask, and Bolan followed his example, wishing he had goggles to protect his eyes, as well. Too late. They would make do with what they had, or they would die.

It was a relatively simple choice.

Approaching four, Deckard reached underneath his jacket and produced an Ingram MAC-10 submachine gun, nose-heavy with a fat sound suppressor in a heat-resistant sleeve of fabric. Drawing back the bolt to load and cock the little room broom, Deckard cast a sidelong glance at Bolan, smiling as he did so.

"Ready?"

"As I'll ever be," Bolan replied.

The elevator door swooshed open to reveal a lobby, slightly larger than the average walk-in closet. To their right, on Deckard's side, a sentry had his metal folding chair propped back against the wall, reading a girlie magazine. It had to have been a good one, for he obviously missed the noisy elevator coming up and seemed surprised when it disgorged its two armed passengers.

The sentry tried to save himself but was too late. He dropped the magazine and pushed forward in his chair, his right hand flailing toward a short pump-action shotgun braced against the wall. He nearly had it when a short burst from the Ingram ripped across his chest and dropped him on his left side in a boneless sprawl.

"Through there," Deckard said, pointing with his weapon to the only door in sight.

Instead of waiting for the Executioner to move, Deckard stepped forward, kicked it in and followed through, with Bolan on his heels. Already leaning toward conviction that the man was really on his side—or else, one hell of a demented method actor—Bolan had him covered as they burst into the cutting plant.

A quick scan showed him all the necessary detail of the room. One long, cafeteria-style table set directly in the middle of the floor, with half a dozen characters in white lab coats milling around, attending Bunsen burners, scales and bubbling flasks. Two hardmen dressed in well-cut suits were covering the operation, one on either side, both armed with AK-47s slung on shoulder straps. Away to Bolan's left-hand side, the far end of the room, light spilled in through an open door, and he could see more figures moving, though he had no time to make a head count or decide what they were doing.

Bolan had the nearer of the two guards sighted as the guy reacted, swiveling to bring them under fire, his AK sliding off its sling and into ready hands as if he had rehearsed the move a thousand times. In fact, he may have done just that, but he was still too late to save himself.

The Uzi stuttered, six or seven Parabellum manglers chewing up the hardman's chest, releasing an explosive crimson spray from heart and lungs. The guy was dead before he knew it, but that didn't stop his index finger's progress as it clenched around the AK's trigger, spraying bullets toward the ceiling and unleashing streams of chalky plaster dust as he sprawled backward, slack in death.

Deckard's Ingram marked the passing of the second guard, who jerked through a spastic little dance before his legs got tangled up together and he went down in a heap. His automatic rifle clattered on the floor, unused, and spun away beneath the table, several paces to his left.

There was a blur of movement, startled voices barking from the bright adjacent room, and Bolan swung in that direction, covering the doorway with his Uzi, ready for the backup shooters when they came. A crash of glass and submachine-gun fire announced his brother's entry to the skirmish, and the Executioner was stepping in that direction, to help Johnny, when the loud crack of a pistol shot surprised him, and a bullet sizzled past his face.

He spun back toward the table stacked with lab equipment, just in time to see the white coats drawing pistols. Every one of them was armed, it seemed, but at the moment, Bolan had to think about only one of them.

Tall and rangy, with his frizzy hair grown out to shoulder length, the man was coming straight at Bolan with a wild expression on his face, a stainless-steel revolver aimed at Bolan's chest.

DECKARD HADN'T expected any of the lab technicians to be armed. It was a deviation from the norm, but one he should have made allowance for, and he cursed his inattention to detail as pistols suddenly appeared in every hand.

The first shot startled Deckard, even then. The tall gunner with the fright wig was apparently some kind of quick-draw artist, maybe fantasized about moonlighting as a hit man when he wasn't cutting heroin. He was fast, the shiny handgun leaping from its holster on his belt and hammering a shot toward Evan Green, before Deckard was even conscious of the fellow moving.

He had to get his act together, dammit! Deckard cursed himself, and swung his MAC-10's heavy muzzle toward the scarecrow figure, just as Green became aware that he was under fire.

Too late? How many rounds did he have left? The Ingram ran through ammo at an awesome cyclic rate of some 1,200 rounds per minute, and the largest magazine available held only thirty-two rounds—call it a second and a half of steady fire before he needed to reload. If Deckard's piece was empty, it could mean the end of Evan Green, and if he couldn't reach his backup weapon fast enough, perhaps his end, as well.

Screw it!

He squeezed the Ingram's trigger, felt a satisfying shudder as the stubby SMG ran through its last rounds in a heartbeat, dead on target. The lab tech had left his right flank totally exposed, his arm raised to sight along the stubby barrel of his handgun, and the bullets opened up his side as if he had a zipper sewn below his arm. His second shot went wild, and he went down, Green nodding swift acknowledgment as Deckard swung around to face the five remaining guns.

His SMG was definitely empty now, and groping for a fresh mag in his pockets was the shortest route to sudden death that he could think of. Rather than reload the Ingram,

Deckard let it go and dropped into a fighting crouch, his Glock in hand almost before he had a chance to will it, instinct and rehearsal taking over in the crunch.

The pistol had no sound suppressor, but there had been enough wild firing in the lab already to alert whichever neighbors were at home downstairs. The last thing that concerned him at the moment was the prospect of police arriving on the scene. A person had to be alive to get arrested, and if Deckard was too slow in his reaction to the present threat, the question would be moot.

Five lab techs left, and three of them were swinging their pistols toward Deckard as he framed the nearest—thus most dangerous—of their number in his sights. He used the classic double tap, two shots in rapid fire, released so quickly that, at least in theory, there was no time for the recoil of the first shot to screw up the shooter's aim on the second.

This time, at least, the theory seemed to work.

His human target took both hollowpoint rounds dead center in the chest, his white coat splashed with scarlet as he staggered backward, stout legs turned to rubber that wouldn't support his weight. He sat down hard, the impact of his backside on the floor expelling blood from mouth and nostrils, then he toppled slowly onto his back.

Before his rear made contact with the floor, Deckard had tracked the Glock a few degrees off to his right to find another target. This one had him lined up, squinting down the barrel of what looked to be a Luger, both hands wrapped around the piece to hold it steady.

They fired together, Deckard slumping to the left but holding steady on his mark, the hardman's bullet scorching through the dead air where his face had been a heartbeat earlier. The Glock spoke twice, but dodging that incoming round had partly queered his aim. One round slapped into the gunner's stomach, just above his belt line, while the other missed completely.

The gut shot did it, though, as sloppy as it was. The shooter doubled over with a breathless gasp of pain, dropping his pistol, both hands clutching at his wounded abdomen. Not necessarily a fatal wound, but Deckard fixed that, squeezing off a third round from the floor. It drilled the shooter's balding scalp and dropped him where he stood, his limbs splayed at awkward angles.

Three left, and even as the thought took form, he heard Green's Uzi stuttering away at them, saw one of the white coats reeling backward, his arms raised in a futile effort to protect himself from automatic fire. When he went down, one elbow caught the near end of the table and the table's folding legs collapsed, the burners, beakers, bags of dope and all the rest of it cascading toward the chemist's stricken figure.

A stray round from the Uzi struck one of those plastic bags, and it began to snow inside the lab, Deckard recoiling from the sudden blizzard. Thankful for the mask, he squinted, raised an arm to shield his eyes, as he backpedaled from the roiling cloud of snow-white death. He triggered two quick shots at nothing in particular and felt an urge to laugh out loud, a moment of hysteria, as he imagined fighting for his life inside a giant snowy globe.

He was aware of Evan Green still firing, somewhere to his right. Another lab tech going down, this one with only half a face, scalp flapping with the bullets' impact like a cheap toupee.

And that left one, besides the unknown backup force next door, apparently engaged by Gray. The bastard could be anywhere, the million-dollar smoke screen hiding him from Deckard at the moment—and from Green as well, apparently; no sputter from the Uzi—but the only exits from the room were covered, so the white coat wasn't going anywhere.

Taking advantage of the momentary lull, Deckard sidestepped, reclaimed his Ingram, dumped its empty magazine and snapped a fresh one into place. He jacked a round into the chamber, held the submachine gun ready as he put the Glock back in its holster.

Time to rock and roll.

He faded to his left, away from Green, trying to make it look as if the door was open and uncovered. It would take an idiot to fall for that, of course—unless the guy was desperate, scared out of his mind and grasping at the flimsiest of straws.

He heard the wild man coming, winding up his battle cry until it sounded like a siren coming through the snow storm. Deckard had his Ingram braced and ready when the guy came into view, charging directly toward the open door and wailing like a banshee as he came.

Which didn't make the semiauto pistol in his hand any less dangerous.

The lab tech flung his gun arm toward Deckard, squeezing off in rapid fire, the *pop-pop* of his weapon sounding like a .32-caliber, or maybe a .380-caliber pistol. Call the piece a lady's gun, if you were so inclined; a square hit on a vital organ would be every bit as deadly as the mule kick of a .44 Magnum.

Deckard stroked the Ingram's trigger and released it quickly to avoid expending his whole magazine. He saw the bullets strike home in a blur of motion, his target lurching, breaking stride, the man's war cry smothered by a gurgling sound that seemed to echo from his chest and throat, both at once. Already dead or on his way, the guy kept firing as he fell, but he was long past aiming and wasted bullets knocking divots from the floor and walls.

He didn't know how many rounds the hardman had absorbed, but from the Ingram's rate of fire and the amount of blood in evidence, Deckard supposed it may have been as much as half a magazine. At least a dozen rounds, for sure, and that meant he had one or two more bursts, if he was lucky, before he had to reload once again.

How many shooters in the other room with Johnny Gray? Too many, from the sound of things. So what?

He didn't want to live forever, anyway. Deckard moved swiftly toward the battleground next door.

CLIMBING THE FIRE escape had been a good idea, but it had not delivered Johnny to the point he had expected. Peering through a dirty windowpane, he counted five men, all but one of them in shirtsleeves, four of them with pistols in plain sight, the fifth sporting a bulge beneath his tailored jacket where the shoulder holster ought to be. Besides the handguns, he saw other hardware close at hand: two submachine guns lying on a countertop to his right, beside a coffee urn; a riot shotgun and an Armalite assault rifle standing off to one side, propped up against the wall.

The men were playing cards, though Johnny didn't recognize the game. There was an open door behind the farthest of them, but he had no view of the adjoining room. No drug lab visible from where he crouched in darkness, and he had experienced another pang of doubt. Suppose it was a trap, no lab at all, just shooters waiting for their targets to arrive. He had no walkie-talkie with him, no way to alert his brother that he smelled a rat.

But, if those five soldiers were expecting company, would they be playing cards and sipping coffee? Even if they were the second-string reserves, they should be on alert. Deckard would certainly have given them an ETA. Which meant... what?

Johnny checked his watch and saw that he had fifteen seconds left on his original five minutes, until his brother and Deckard made their move. The window kept him from eavesdropping on the men around the table—not that he spoke Russian, anyway—but Johnny reckoned he would hear his brother's entry when it came. If nothing else, he had a clear view of the cardplayers, and their reactions should alert him to the raid in progress.

Johnny started counting down, the numbers running silently inside his head. A beat before he got to "zero," two of the cardplayers bolted from their seats and lunged for nearby weapons, while the other three began to shove back their chairs, craning necks to catch a glimpse of some commotion in the other room. Johnny was rearing back to smash his SMG against the windowpane, when he heard muffled sounds of automatic fire, the telltale noise of a Kalashnikov.

He followed through, the windowpane imploding in a spray of razored fragments, Johnny hacking at the sawtoothed remnants with the muzzle of his weapon. Two of the cardplayers—one still seated, the other already on his feet and brandishing the riot gun—turned toward the window, startled, while the others concentrated on the sounds of combat emanating from the other room.

These boys were good, professional, no doubt about it. The shotgunner had his weapon leveled and was drawing back the slide action to put a live round in the chamber when Johnny nailed him, a quick burst to the chest from his Uzi, taking the shooter down as if yanked by some unseen hand. Even airborne and dying, the guy managed to chamber his round and squeeze the shotgun's trigger, but his angle had changed, the charge of buckshot cracking bricks and mortar a foot above Johnny's head.

Dumb luck had saved him. If the shooter had been five or six yards farther back, the shotgun pellets would have had a chance to spread, one or two of the .33-caliber pellets dropping low enough to drill his forehead. But there was no time to reflect on chance or fate, with four more shooters still alive and kicking in the room, while Johnny crouched outside.

The nearest seated gunner, facing Johnny, had apparently decided not to waste time standing. Instead, he pushed off with his heels and hips, dropped from his chair into a kneeling posture, twisting sideways to reduce the portion of his body offered as a target, even as he sighted down the barrel of his autoloading pistol.

For something like a microsecond, Johnny Gray imagined he could *see* the bullet streaking toward his face, resembling an insect on its dead-end glide path to a speeding windshield. Johnny let his instinct make the call. Instead of ducking backward into darkness, he lunged forward, through the shattered window, slithering across the sill and feeling glass that he had missed etch tracks across his stomach. Johnny also felt a bullet clip his heel, as he kicked upward for the leverage he needed to complete the move.

His elbows banged linoleum before his chest and stomach hit the floor, jarring his Uzi as he triggered off another burst. It spoiled his aim to some extent, but he was so close to his enemy by now that any shots they fired would qualify as point-blank range.

His bullets hit the kneeling gunner in his left thigh, hip and shoulder, not the killing shots Johnny had hoped for, but the impact was enough to rock his adversary and spin him halfway to his left, crying aloud in shock and pain. Still, he was capable of fighting, and his next two bullets peeled back long strips of linoleum a foot from Johnny's face.

The Uzi stammered frantically, and he was back on target now, the shooter twitching in his death throes as he slumped over backward, legs pinned beneath him in what would have been a painful attitude if he were still alive to feel it.

Move!

Someone had reached the Armalite assault rifle, and it was knocking divots from the floor, its zigzag pattern racing toward the point where it would intersect with Johnny's wriggling. It was a waste of precious time and energy to rise, most likely suicidal, so he rolled across the dingy floor, trying to keep the card table between himself and the rifleman, returning fire as best he could.

The table was a mixed blessing. It shielded Johnny from his would-be killer's view, but it was flimsy, made of fiberboard, and bullets easily punched through it. Through those holes Johnny could see his adversary's feet and legs.

Why not?

Still rolling, Johnny fired a burst that clipped the gunner's ankles, rising with the Uzi's recoil to obliterate one kneecap. He expected something in the nature of a scream, but the rifleman's vocal cords were frozen by shock. The wounded man collapsed, his torso smashing hard into the table as he fell, sufficient weight and force applied to bring down the table with him, still serving as a flimsy shield. Unfazed by the obstruction, Johnny fired directly through the tabletop, rewarded with the vision of his adversary's shattered ankles thrashing, leaving crimson streaks on the linoleum before they came to rest.

His ears were ringing from the sound of rapid-fire explosions battering around the room, more combat noises still erupting from what seemed to be a larger room next door. The reek of cordite and the sharp, metallic scent of fresh-spilled blood reminded Johnny of the drug lab they had come to smash, and the surgical mask that still dangled around his neck by its elastic strap, forgotten in his rush to crash the window when the shooting started.

Johnny pulled the mask into place and fished inside his jacket for another magazine to feed the Uzi. Several seconds had elapsed without incoming fire, his two surviving enemies still hidden from him by the bullet-riddled table lying on its side. For a moment Johnny wondered if the last two shooters had gone after his brother and Deckard in the lab. The answer, when it came a heartbeat later, echoed in the sound of submachine guns firing from the doorway of the room in which he lay.

A quick glance toward the nearby counter showed him the matching SMGs were gone, and Johnny put it all together in a flash. The last two cardplayers were firing not at him, but at his brother and the CIA man who had led them to this target in the first place. With a bit more luck, he hoped it would be all the edge he needed to complete his sweep.

Johnny had no idea how long the two gunners would remain oblivious to the destruction of their comrades, but he clearly had no time to waste. He rolled to his left, drew both knees to his chest and pushed off with his free hand, rising to his knees. Ten feet in front of him, the two machine gunners were crouched beside the open doorway, unloading with their MP-5s at targets Johnny couldn't see, although he had no doubt who those targets were.

He never knew what tipped off the gunner. A scraping sound when he rose from the floor, perhaps, or maybe some survival instinct more akin to ESP. Whatever, Johnny had the left-hand gunner in his sights, his finger already taking up the Uzi's trigger slack, when the second gunner glanced backward, saw him kneeling in the middle of the room and called a warning to his comrade as he turned.

Too late.

The shooter on the left side of the doorway took the Uzi burst between his shoulder blades and was punched forward by the impact, sluggishly rebounding after he collided with the doorjamb. Johnny felt, as much as saw, the second gunman pivoting to bring him under fire, uncertain whether he could realign his own sights in the time required to save himself.

And then, before Johnny could fire, the gunner gave a sideways lurch, blood spouting from his neck and face, where silenced rounds had ripped into his flesh. Johnny saw Able Deckard lean in through the doorway, his Ingram outstretched in one hand like an oversized pistol, still spitting rounds into the Russian as he fell.

"You hit?" the man from Langley asked him.

Johnny took a hasty inventory. "Nope."

"Good deal," the other said. "We'd better split before the cops decide to pay a call."

10

The flashing button on his telephone told Hal Brognola that the call was coming in from Stony Man. It was a special line, the only one that bypassed both his secretary and the Justice switchboard operator. The line was as secure as cutting-edge technology could make it—meaning, the big Fed supposed, that some smart-ass in junior-high school could devise a way to eavesdrop on Brognola's calls if he applied himself.

And that was why he always used the scrambler, just in case.

He let it ring twice, picked up on the third, scowling with discomfort at the tight knot in his stomach. How he had avoided ulcers was a mystery.

"Speak to me," he said, no time to waste on pleasantries.

"It's me," Barbara Price informed him.

"What's the scoop?"

"We've got a hot flash from Berlin," she said.

So much for wishful thinking, damm it all. "Is it confirmed?"

"Ninety percent. We're short of witnesses, you understand, but there were three hits overnight, all targets linked to the Valerik Family."

"How many KIA?" Brognola asked, wishing he didn't have to know.

"About two dozen, give or take. The last place, there was some kind of explosion. They're still going through the rubble."

"Jesus H."

He had been hoping that the brothers would lose track of
their intended quarry when he skipped from Amsterdam to
Germany, maybe get tired and come on back to the United
States. To that end, he had ordered Price not to spill the news
about Valerik's latest flight.

For all the good it did, Brognola thought, he might as well
have given them the bastard's forwarding address.

"There was a witness to the second hit," Price said.
"Some kind of night watchman or something. I'm not really
sure."

"Go on." Brognola tried not to snap at her or sound too
impatient as she rambled, plainly nervous.

"Well, we've got an ear with the security detachment over
there, you know. GSG-9?"

"Uh-huh."

"And what they're saying is, this witness counted three
men on the strike."

Brognola blinked at that. "Three *men?*" he pressed. "It
couldn't have been two men and a woman?"

"That's what I asked. Twice, in fact. Guy claims he had
a clear view of three men. No faces, mind you, but he's
positive all three of them were male."

Brognola skulled it over, came up empty. On the off
chance, just in case, he asked, "Are all of ours accounted
for, right now?"

"Affirmative," Price replied. "I double-checked on that
myself."

Thank God for that, at least. If anyone from Able Team
or Phoenix Force had joined the brothers, Brognola knew
they would all be in a world of hurt.

"So, any thoughts on who could be the odd man out?"
he asked.

"We have considered—and dismissed—the possibility that

these strikes might be unrelated to the ones in Amsterdam. It's way too much coincidence.''

"Agreed," Brognola said. "My question stands."

"Assuming that it is the brothers, and they've picked up a third man somewhere along the way," she said, "smart money says he joined the team in Amsterdam. And that suggests—"

"That he could be the one who aimed them toward Berlin," the big Fed finished for her.

"Correct."

"Which means," Brognola continued, now thinking aloud, "that he must be someone with knowledge of Valerik's movements. Call it either some kind of surveillance apparatus, or an eye inside the Family itself."

"I'm leaning toward the first choice," Price said. "No matter how I try, I can't imagine anybody from Valerik's team being able to locate the brothers, much less cut a deal."

"Plus which," Brognola said, "a rat inside the Family would want some kind of payoff, then he'd split. He damn sure wouldn't tag along and help them blitz his buds."

"Assuming Striker even trusted him that much."

"Which he wouldn't." And Brognola's response raised yet another question: who would Bolan trust?

He was effectively cut off from Stony Man, clearly suspicious of Brognola—and the others too, no doubt, by now. Who else would have the intel Bolan needed *and* the wherewithal to win him over, find an active place on Bolan's fighting team?

"Aw, shit!"

"You're thinking—"

"Someone from the Company," he said. "It has to be."

"I'm not so sure," she said. "Cross purposes."

"What else is new?" Brognola challenged. "Christ, with Langley, half the time, the left hand doesn't know there is a right hand, much less what it's doing."

"So, the project may not have unanimous support, then."

The big Fed picked up on the relief in Price's tone and knew that it was premature. "That doesn't help us any," he replied. "We need to know which way the heavies lean, and who the players are. Until we pin that down, we're whistling in the dark."

"It's good to feel like whistling, though," she said.

"Just don't get used to it."

"I'm only saying—"

"I know what you're saying." Brognola deliberately cut her off, crushing her hopes. "It changes nothing."

The ringing silence on her end was like a slap across Brognola's face. When Price spoke again, her voice was distant, with a trace of frost around the edges. "So," she said, "the orders stand."

"If I rescind them, you'll be the first to know," Brognola said.

"And if, by chance, we hear from someone in Berlin?"

"You tell him nothing, trace the call if possible, and then report to me immediately."

"Right," she said. And then, as if for emphasis, "Yes, sir."

"You know I—"

He was talking to the dial tone, startled by the fact that she had cut him off. First time for everything, he told himself, and wondered if she would obey her orders when it counted.

Yes.

She understood what was at stake, what she would jeopardize by following her heart instead of standing orders. Barbara Price was a professional, above all else. When push came to shove, he trusted her to stick.

Price wasn't his problem at the moment. He was more concerned about the strange report of a third man traveling—and fighting—with the Bolan brothers in Berlin. Who was he? How could Brognola find out?

The possibilities were limited. Finding a competent shooter was no great problem, all things considered, and the world was no doubt filled with people who despised the Russian Mafia. The rub came when you tried to find someone who didn't mind the odds—what was it now, something like three against three thousand?—which the Bolan brothers were confronting in their private war with the Valerik Family. And those odds didn't even count the spooky hangers-on, either from Langley or the Russian side.

Thinking of Langley brought him back to the idea that Mr. X himself might be connected to the CIA. Why not? It wouldn't be the first time that the Company, with all its airtight need-to-know compartments had found its several units working at cross purposes. Forget about the mole hunts. Langley had enough trouble making sure its paymaster wasn't supporting some foreign regime that its field agents were trying to destabilize. There didn't even have to be a schism in the Agency, since one group—at least theoretically—would never even know the other's goals.

And Brognola, of course, was frozen out of both, except when he was briefed, or when someone at the Farm hacked into the Company's computer data banks. Right now, he felt as if he were groping in a fog so thick he couldn't see his hand six inches from his nose. It was a claustrophobic, almost suffocating sense of helplessness that left him feeling useless.

And that, in turn, could only piss him off.

Brognola wished the brothers and their newfound sidekick would give up the fight. In all the time that he had known Mack Bolan, Brognola had never seen him back down from a fight or quit the field before an issue was decided. Regardless of the cost, once Bolan took on a mission, he inevitably saw it through.

Brognola had considered pulling rank, but he'd decided it would never work. Bolan would want to know his reasons, wouldn't settle for a brush-off, and if Brognola broke confidence, explained himself, there was at least a fifty-fifty chance that the soldier still would go ahead regardless.

What could he have done in that case?

What could he do now?

The choice of action he had chosen was already proving dangerous enough. If Bolan felt compelled to break with Stony Man, there would be hell to pay on more levels than Brognola cared to think about. It would include the Oval Office, and that scenario made him wish he could simply run away and hide somewhere until the storm had spent itself and clearance of the rubble had begun.

Fat chance.

One trait Brognola shared with Bolan was his stubborn inability to quit once he had joined a cause. Barring a miracle he couldn't foresee, he seemed to be on a hard collision course with Bolan and his allies somewhere down the road.

Brognola cherished no illusions as to what would happen if he opened up hostilities against the Bolan brothers. All the time that he had hunted Bolan, in the bad old days when the Executioner waged a one-man war against the Mafia, the big Fed had been close to nailing him a time or two, but never pulled it off. Not with the FBI behind him, and his target's face plastered all over Wanted posters, newspaper front pages and the TV news. If he had to repeat that exercise today, Brognola couldn't even wield the weapon of publicity.

Bolan was "dead." Brognola had arranged that scam himself, planned every detail to the nth degree, and if he blew the whistle on himself, who would believe it? Stripping Bolan of his cover meant destroying everything the SOG Director had built and worked for during recent years, the team at Stony Man, their mission, all of it.

But hunting Bolan on his own, Brognola realized, would have the same result. Some of his people might defect to Bolan's side, but even if they opted for neutrality, Brognola reckoned several of them—probably the ones he needed most—would definitely quit the team.

As for Brognola, if the Bolan brothers started tracking him, his days were numbered. Even if he built himself an igloo in the frozen heartland of Antarctica, subsisting on a snow-and-blubber diet, he would still go mad before a year was out, jumping at every shadow, waiting for the crosshairs to line up, the killing shot to take him down.

"How did we come to this?" Brognola asked himself, surprised to find that he had actually voiced the question. Knowing, even as he did so, that it was the wrong question.

It didn't matter how he'd gotten where he was.

What mattered, now, was getting out alive.

IN NOBLE PRUETT'S office, thumbtacked to the wall, where he could see it from his desk, there was a poster with a photo of a wild-eyed lunatic bound in a straitjacket. The caption read: Paranoia Is Simply A State of Heightened Awareness.

He kept that truth in mind as he made one more circuit of the block, checking for shadows, spotting none, then pulled into the parking lot of the convenience store he had selected. It was midday in McLean, Virginia, two miles west of Langley. There were people moving in and out of the convenience store, but Pruett didn't mind. He wanted people, needed them for cover, so he wouldn't be the only one around and thereby stick in anybody's mind.

The two pay phones out front were free as Pruett nosed his nondescript car to the curb in front of them. The vehicle was borrowed, one more layer of insulation, just in case. He stepped out of the car, moved toward the telephones and glanced around to make sure no one saw him as he palmed a Post-It note and stuck it onto one phone, covering the coin slot. Printed on the square of paper in block letters, was the message Out of Order. Pruett took the second handset from its cradle, punched in digits for a credit card that didn't bear his name, then thirteen more for his connection overseas. He had both numbers memorized.

Waiting for his call to ring through on the transatlantic side, he felt another wave of irritation coming on, but managed to suppress it with a bit of willpower. He had been fuming for the best part of an hour, off and on, beginning when he got the message from his secretary that his cousin Rick had called while he was in a meeting with the deputy director, asking Pruett to return his call as soon as possible.

A number had been left for him, but Pruett didn't bother reading it. He had no cousin Rick—a tag that he had fabricated for Vassily Krestyanov—and Pruett knew the number had been picked at random from some local telephone directory. Instead, he would be calling Europe, using this month's contact number for the Russian, but he couldn't do it from his office—nowhere from the Company complex, in fact.

So, he had gone "to lunch" with borrowed wheels—a simple lie about his own car stalling out—and put Langley behind him, driving to McLean. No one had followed him, as far as he could tell, and while the line wasn't secure, per se, he had no reason to believe the public telephones at this particular convenience store were being monitored.

A strange voice answered on the other end—he'd never heard the same one twice; some kind of cutout number, he supposed—and Pruett offered this week's password. Fifteen seconds later, Krestyanov himself was on the line.

"You had no difficulty getting out to call?" the Russian asked.

"It's always difficult," Pruett replied. "What's so important that you had to call me at the office?"

"Our associate is still beset by problems, even after changing domiciles," Krestyanov said. Translation: Valerik's ass was in a sling. His enemies had somehow followed him, despite the jump from Amsterdam to Germany.

"Sounds like that move may not have been the best idea,"

Pruett replied. It had been Krestyanov's idea, of course, and he couldn't resist acknowledging the fact.

"There is, in fact, another problem," Krestyanov informed him.

"Hey, more trouble," Pruett muttered. "There's a huge surprise." In fact, the past two weeks or so, there had been nothing but bad news, one crisis after another, making Pruett wish that he had never helped devise the scheme at all. It had seemed relatively simple, then. The next best thing to foolproof.

Now…

"You don't wish to be informed?" the Russian chided him.

"I'm here. I'm listening. Get on with it."

"There are at least three members of the opposition in Berlin," the Russian said. "All seem to be Americans. Unfortunately, they are unidentified."

"Can't help you there," Pruett said. "If you had clear photos, maybe, but the risk would be tremendous."

"Please remember your priorities."

"My first priority is staying out of federal prison. Get it? Anyway, I told you, if you don't have photographs or something else, like maybe fingerprints or DNA, there's nothing I can do, at any price."

"Next time," Krestyanov said, "I'll have our friend request that the assassins pose for snapshots and provide a urine sample."

"Hey, it couldn't hurt," Pruett said, more than equal to the task of matching Krestyanov's snide tone. "Of course, it doesn't matter what you've got, unless they're in the system—and a check means hacking into Justice, while we're at it. Better just to grease them and be done with it."

"Unfortunately, they appear to be professionals. They also seem unusually well informed about our comrade's travel plans. Would you have any thoughts on that?"

"Like what?" He didn't like the Russian's tone, almost accusatory, certainly insinuating. "Are you hinting that I've got a leak at this end?"

He could almost see Krestyanov shrug, the affectation of a casual demeanor. "Anything is possible," the former KGB man said.

"If I were you, I'd look a little closer to the action for my suspects, if you follow me. I'm not the one who made his travel plans."

"I will be checking every possibility," Krestyanov said. "If you are wise, you'll do the same."

"No need. I've only got two people here with any working knowledge of our understanding, as it is, and neither one of them was briefed about the move to Germany."

"So," Krestyanov replied, "you are the only one who knew our friend was on his way to Germany?"

"The only one on *my* team," Pruett said, correcting him. Another damned insinuation. He was sick of it. "I don't suppose you ever stopped to think that maybe this is all *his* fault? I never saw an operation like the one he runs that didn't have its share of rats."

"He has assured me—"

"Let me guess," Pruett answered, interrupting Krestyanov. "He swears his guys are clean. They're all blood brothers, and he trusts them with his life."

"He trusts no one at this point."

"Maybe with good reason," Pruett said.

"Before you cut me off, I was about to say that he's assured me no one knew about the move."

"No one? You're telling me he's traveling alone?"

"No one except his chief lieutenant and his bodyguards," the Russian replied.

"That makes, what? Six or seven guys, at least?"

"We must not close our minds to other possibilities," Krestyanov said.

And Pruett knew exactly what he meant. The Company was like one of those Russian dolls that opened up to reveal a smaller one inside, another inside that, and so on, each one intricately carved and painted in precise detail. At Langley, you could never really tell for sure what anybody else was thinking, who they might be working for behind the scenes. Pruett had covered all the bases he could think of, swept his tracks, but there was still a chance that he had missed something, someone.

It still might turn around and bite him on the ass.

He didn't like to think about that, understandably, but there was no avoiding it, especially when things went seriously wrong, like now. A part of him was moved to wish that he could cut his losses, leave Krestyanov and Valerik twisting in the wind, but it was too damned late for that.

And there was too damned much at stake, too much for him to gain if they could pull it off as planned.

"I'll try to check around," he said at last, reluctantly. "It won't be easy, though."

"Of course not. If you find something…"

"I'll let you know. And handle it myself."

"We're getting close," the Russian said. "So very close."

"I hear you."

"And I hope to hear from you. Good news next time, perhaps?"

"We'll see."

He hung up the receiver, took the sticky Out of Order note and dropped it in a nearby garbage can before returning to his car. He would pursue a different evasive route on his way back to Langley, trying to decide the safest, surest way to learn if he was blown.

The only proof, of course, would be when they arrested him. For that, they needed evidence, a warrant, witnesses— the whole nine yards. The fact that he was still at liberty proved nothing, but he had been careful, dammit! If the bastards knew what he was up to, if they even guessed at part of it, why wasn't he in jail? Or maybe dead?

Any trial would be such an embarrassment to all concerned that Pruett wouldn't put it past them to arrange some kind of fatal "accident." He was perpetually on guard, but there were ways to do it, even so. No one could check under his hood and crawl around beneath the chassis *every* time he drove his car. To survive, he had to be alert *and* lucky, every single day.

The opposition only needed to get lucky once.

The drive back to his office from McLean may not have been the best time to imagine someone fiddling with his car. Of course, he wasn't riding in his car, which helped Pruett relax for six or seven seconds. Then, he saw the semi rig ahead of him, another coming up behind, and started fantasizing demolition-derby plots, with long-haul spooks pulled in to waste him on the highway. Who would ever know the difference, when there were eighty to a hundred traffic deaths across the country every single day?

The semi at his back drew closer, then changed lanes and rumbled past him, Pruett braced for impact until the rig was half a mile in front of him and well away.

Sometimes paranoia wasn't any help.

Pruett had spent his adult life immersed in secrets, lies, deception, covert power plays. Sometimes the action led to killing, though it frankly wasn't all that common. He had ordered two—no, three—deaths on his own initiative to date, not counting the anticipated contract on Ted Williams, out in Arizona, that was canceled when the bastard turned up dead. The thought of someone writing up his execution order seemed unreal, but Pruett knew that he couldn't dismiss it out of hand.

The only way he could protect himself, beyond all doubt, was to continue on the present course until he was victorious. At that point, Pruett would become untouchable.

THE FIRST TIME Hargus Webber ran for public office, he was barely old enough to vote himself. It was a small-town city council seat, and he had lost the race, but came back strong to win it two years later. And he had been winning ever since.

All but the prize he coveted above all things in heaven or on earth. The one thing he would give his soul for, if he still had one to trade away.

The White House had eluded him thus far, though he remained a senior member of the U.S. Senate, chairing or participating in four of the top six committees. Last time around in the primary races, he had come so close to carrying Wisconsin for his party, but the bastards snuck around behind his back and stole it from him at the finish line. Webber had taken his humiliation gracefully—he was nothing, if not a gentleman—but he had also started taking names, remembering the faces and the sins of those who screwed him over.

It was quite a list, and he was looking forward to the day when it was payback time.

Not long, he told himself.

There was a Senate vote that afternoon on some new gun-control provision of the latest half-assed "crime bill," and the senator had been deliberating graceful ways to dodge it when the call from Noble Pruett got him off the hook. The last thing Webber needed at the moment was a controversy, lousy columnists attacking him because they thought he either loved or hated guns.

The truth was that he didn't give a shit.

Forget about the goddamned guns, he told himself, and settled back into the comfort of his chauffeured limousine. His driver carried one, of course, because he also served as Webber's bodyguard—important people had to watch themselves, these days—but Webber didn't think the current diversion would require a show of marksmanship.

Their destination was an intimate, expensive restaurant off Military Road in Arlington. The place had private banquet rooms available, and Pruett would be waiting for him there, to break his latest news of their cooperative venture. Webber feared the news wouldn't be good, but he resolved to wait and see. There was no point in worrying before he knew the worst. God knew his hair was white enough already, and he didn't want to see it falling out in clumps from too much stress.

Who ever saw the President of the United States in a toupee?

As far as Webber knew, the plan had run like clockwork up to now. They were on schedule, all the pieces falling into place, and he had even come to terms with his initial squeamishness about The Incident that had to precede his final victory. The more he thought about it, Webber had begun to see it as a small price for the nation, an investment in procuring the greatest President and statesman within living memory.

No one had ever challenged Hargus Webber with an accusation of false modesty.

He felt the limo slowing, glanced through the nearest tinted window and discovered they had reached the restaurant. Zoned out there, for a minute, Webber thought, and quickly shook it off. He wasn't getting senile, dammit, just because his smart-ass thirty-two-year-old opponent tried to spread that vicious rumor when he ran for reelection, back in '96. Webber had shown the grinning prick a thing or two about what was needed in a down-and-dirty Senate race. The photographs of Mr. Clean cavorting with a black transvestite in a cheap motel were never traced to Webber, but they sent him back to Washington for six more years.

He did what was necessary, and he didn't look back.

Webber's driver held the door for him, followed him inside and split off when the hostess greeted them, detouring toward the lounge, where he would drink coffee and wait. The hostess seemed to recognize him, but she didn't ask, and Webber didn't volunteer.

"I'm meeting Mr. Flagg," he told the smiling redhead. "I believe he booked one of your banquet rooms."

"Yes, sir. If you'll just follow me."

"Delighted," Webber said, and so he was. It made him feel a decade younger, just to watch her buttocks move inside the short, tight skirt. He felt a stirring, but dismissed it.

This wasn't playtime.

Pruett stood to greet him, as the hostess showed him into their sequestered dining room. They made small talk until the waitress brought their drinks and took their luncheon orders.

When they were alone, he looked around the room and said, "I don't suppose there would be any bugs in here."

"I checked," Pruett said. "We're all right."

"What's the big emergency?"

"It may be nothing, Senator, but I thought I should keep you in the picture, since you've got so much at stake."

"We both do, Mr. Pruett," Webber said, reminding him again that shit would always run downhill.

"Of course. That's what I meant to say."

"By all means, then, what's on your mind?"

"Well, as I said, it may be nothing." Pruett hesitated, frowning.

"But…?"

"The Russians have encountered some resistance on their end," the man from Langley said. "They've had some losses."

"What? In Moscow?" Webber felt a sudden need to gulp down his vodka.

"No, no. Not those Russians. The middlemen."

"The gangsters." Webber frowned, as if the word had left him with a bad taste in his mouth.

"That's right."

"They haven't been discovered?"

"No." Pruett considered it, and then repeated, "No. It's something else, I'm sure."

"Well, what, for God's sake?"

"They've sustained a series of attacks," Pruett answered, "both here—"

"In Washington?"

"The States—Los Angeles, New York—and elsewhere, sir."

"Where else?"

"Canada, the Netherlands, I think. If I remember right, there was some mention of Berlin."

"Attacks, you said?"

"Yes, sir. There have been casualties. A large number."

"People have been killed?" It startled Webber, even knowing as he did the details of their plan, its grim, inevitable outcome.

"Yes, sir."

"What does it have to do with me? With us?"

"It may be nothing," Pruett said. "These people are… well…they have enemies, you understand. It's part of life. When they have disagreements in their line of business, they don't go to court."

"But now, of all times? Are you sure—"

"I'm looking into it," Pruett replied, interrupting him. "As soon as I know any more, you'll be the first to know."

"How many dead so far?" Webber inquired.

"I didn't ask, but it's several dozen, I believe."

"Several dozen? Jesus Chri—"

The waitress entered with their meals and Webber's mouth snapped shut, conditioned reflex twisting it into a smile of sorts. Once they were served and had assured the earnest redhead that they needed nothing more, once she was gone, Webber leaned forward, careful not to let his necktie drag across his plate.

"You can't mean *dozens!*"

"It's what I was told, sir."

"But...I would have heard about it, wouldn't I?"

"The broadcasts have been pretty much restricted to the areas affected," Pruett said. "It's going down as gangsters killing one another, so the networks aren't concerned. No high-school shootings, no racial minorities involved. The Russian Mob's been covered pretty thoroughly, in fact. This may inspire some new think pieces, down the road, but for the moment I believe we're clear."

The senator let that sink in, already looking for the bright side of the situation. All of life was politics. You simply had to know your way around.

"I still expect results," he said at last.

"Yes, sir. So do we all."

"If someone tries to screw me on this deal, I don't intend to take it lying down."

"No, sir. That's not about to happen."

"Well, then," said the man who would be President, "what's all the fuss about?"

11

The beer garden on Tempelhoffer Damm wouldn't be crowded for another hour yet, but patrons had begun to filter in by the time Vassily Krestyanov arrived, with the giant Nikolai Lukasha in tow. They made an odd couple, most definitely worth a second glance, but brimming pitchers full of beer would help the novelty wear off in record time, distracting those among the other patrons who might be inclined to stare.

Manfred Berghoff was waiting for them, holding down a corner booth where they could speak in something that approximated privacy. The polka band was warming up and seemed to have two volume levels: loud and extra loud. Krestyanov knew it would be difficult for anyone in the adjoining booth to overhear their conversation if they exercised some care and didn't get into a shouting match.

Why should they? They were old friends, after all.

"Vassily! Nikolai!" Berghoff stood to greet them, shaking each man's hand in turn.

"Manfred, you're looking well," Krestyanov said, shading the truth a little for the sake of courtesy. In truth, Berghoff didn't look well. He had a vampire's wan complexion, emphasized by the expansive dome of hairless scalp. He had no eyebrows, either—and, if one were so inclined to look, no eyelashes. Hereditary alopecia had deprived Berghoff of every single body hair, from head to toe, but he didn't appear to mind.

"I am well," the German said, nodding toward the booth. "Please, sit. Sit! I've taken the liberty of ordering for all of us."

Two massive pitchers occupied the table, one filled to the brim with yellow lager, the second with the dark beer Lukasha preferred. The giant claimed it for himself as he sat down, filling an empty mug and draining it in one long swallow.

The German's black-on-black ensemble, leather jacket over turtleneck and tailored slacks, with waffle-stomper boots, seemed to exaggerate his baldness, making him the quintessential Nazi skinhead. There was a delicious irony to that, considering the years Berghoff had spent defending communism in East Germany, as an assassin and interrogator for the dreaded Stasi network, but he mirrored the defunct Gestapo's zeal for spilling blood and causing pain. Krestyanov wondered if it might be something in the German water that produced such men...or, maybe, in the beer.

"I was afraid someone had scooped you up, Vassily," Berghoff said. A foam mustache from his beer provided an illusion of whiskers, there and gone as he wiped his mouth with the back of a hand.

"They haven't got me yet," Krestyanov said. "But there's a problem, Manfred. I cannot deny it."

"So this isn't a social call? You need someone eliminated?"

The German's face cracked open in a grin, exposing dentures of the cheapest quality, the teeth resembling off-white counter tiles. According to the standard rumor, Berghoff had fallen under suspicion of treason during one of Stasi's periodic purges. He was innocent, of course, but that meant less than nothing in East Germany, so he had planned to fake his death in an explosion, leave a corpse behind and vanish to the west. To that end, Berghoff found a homosexual about his size and weight, invited the man home for sex and laced his wine with a fast-acting toxin. Afterward, Berghoff had shaved the corpse completely, pulled the stranger's teeth and flushed them down the toilet. It wasn't enough, of course— he couldn't simply leave a toothless corpse for the authorities to find—so he had pulled his own teeth, too, and stuffed them in the dead man's mouth, so the explosion, when it came, would scatter them convincingly around his flat.

The joke: before he had a chance to stage the bombing, Berghoff learned that he wasn't a suspect, after all. In fact, his own immediate superior had been exposed as an informer for the CIA. Berghoff was offered his position and could barely mumble thanks around his mutilated, seeping gums. Before he could accept the grand promotion, though, Bergh-off still had some housecleaning to do. He'd bundled up the body, dumped it in the river and had flushed his own teeth down the toilet, to be rid of them. The dentures he had or-dered took a week to fabricate but looked as if they had been thrown together in five minutes by a child.

"There is someone," Krestyanov said. "Well, more than one, it would appear."

"Terrific!" Berghoff flashed his dentures, took a slug of beer and belched with gusto. "Who are they, these walking corpses?"

"That's the problem, Manfred. I don't know their names."

"No matter," the German replied. "All I need are pho-tographs, addresses."

Krestyanov could only shake his head. "I have no pho-tographs, no addresses."

Still grinning, Berghoff said, "Are they at least in Ger-many, these phantoms? Or am I required to chase them all around the world?"

"They're in Berlin," Lukasha said. "We have descriptions of a sort. Three men, at least. They are well armed and dangerous."

Berghoff considered this news for a moment, then he

snapped his fingers. "Bruck Strasse! Yes? And the whorehouse on Schonhauser Allee? The warehouse on Kottbusser Damm?"

"You're still a sharp one, Manfred." Krestyanov hoped flattery would dam the flow of questions he expected, but the German didn't seem to care how Krestyanov and Lukasha might be connected to the workings of the Russian Mafia.

Instead, he simply asked, "Are they your countrymen?"

Krestyanov shook his head. "Americans, I think, or maybe Britons."

"I think Americans," Lukasha said.

"It's perfect, then!" Berghoff said, showing off his horrid dentures with a smile that split his face almost from ear to ear. "I can't remember the last time I hunted an American. But I enjoyed it. I remember that!"

"These men aren't spies, Manfred. They're soldiers. Maybe mercenaries."

"All the better!" Berghoff said, draining his mug and reaching for the pitcher to refill it. "I was never all that fond of hunting men who don't fight back. Interrogating them, now that's another story. When they squeal—"

"You've brought us to the second part of my request," Krestyanov interrupted. "You're still a clever one, Manfred."

"There's more?"

"If possible," the Russian said, "I'd like for you to capture one of them alive, discover who they are, who sent them here, the usual."

"A double treat, then! Honestly, Vassily, this will be such fun that I'm reluctant to discuss a price."

Krestyanov beat him to the punch. "But you're a businessman, of course."

"I knew you'd understand," the German said. "If I could hunt them on my own, perhaps...but three men, maybe more? I'll need a few assistants. Good ones, if these Yanks are all you claim.''

Krestyanov saw no point in playing games, especially if it would jeopardize the hunt. "They've killed no less than fifty men, in less than two weeks' time," he said.

"Not all in Germany!"

"Most recently in Amsterdam," Krestyanov said. "Before that, in America."

Berghoff digested that for several moments, chasing it with beer, before he said, "I'll use six men, to start. With any luck, I won't need more. The price will sound exorbitant."

"What is the price?" Krestyanov pressed.

Berghoff pretended to consider it some more, then scrunched his face into a rueful mask and named a figure. It was quite a reasonable price. In fact, he had expected Berghoff would demand a good deal more. Still, Krestyanov played out his part, frowning, finally relenting.

"Well," he said, "if that's your best price—"

"You're robbing me, I promise you!"

"Then *you* supply the hardware, Manfred."

"Certainly! A craftsman always brings his tools along."

They shook hands all around to seal the bargain, then Berghoff produced a cellular phone, snapped it open, punched some buttons on the keypad and began to speak in rapid German, giving orders. Krestyanov, who spoke six languages with perfect fluency, took in the brief, one-sided conversation.

"No problems, then?" Krestyanov asked.

"No problems," Berghoff said. "You'll get your scalps."

"And one live prisoner. Remember that, Manfred."

"If possible," the German said.

"Of course. If you could, it might be worth a bonus."

"A live one, then. So it is written, so it shall be done. Trust me!"

"You've never failed me, Manfred."

"Of course not," Berghoff answered, puffing out his ample chest. "I am the best!"

I hope so, thought the Russian colonel, as he sipped his beer. For all our sakes.

CHRISTIAN KEANE had never been much of a diplomat. On balance, he was too straightforward and plainspoken, some said tactless, and he had been known to ruffle feathers when a song-and-dance routine was needed to assuage bruised egos. This problem being recognized by Noble Pruett, Keane was no longer dispatched on missions that required negotiating skills.

And there was nothing to negotiate with his intended targets in Berlin. His mission was to track them down and rub them out, as quickly and efficiently as possible.

Of course, before he could complete that chore, Keane had to find out who they were.

He checked his watch and verified his premonition that the Russian would be late. Keane wished that he had been dispatched to Amsterdam instead of Germany. He could have killed some time relaxing in the red-light district while he waited for his contact to arrive instead of loitering around a smoky bar where red-faced older men appeared to be intent on seeing who could choke down the most beer before he burst.

The giant wandered in three minutes later, almost fifteen minutes late. He was impossible to miss, the way he had to stoop to clear the doorway, and a couple of the wilder drunks were grinning at him, whispering to their companions. They had something on their sodden minds, some kind of prank or insult, maybe. Keane wished they would go ahead with it, but cooler heads prevailed after the giant glanced in their direction, flexing shoulders that were broad enough to strain his custom-tailored jacket. One look in the giant's eyes, and the potential pranksters felt a sudden need for more cold beer.

Lukasha had him spotted, moving through the crowd at will, the portly drinkers giving way in front of him. It had been eighteen months, at least, since Keane had seen the Russian, but the big man still remembered him.

So far, so good.

Keane didn't stand, though it would've been courteous to do so. In Keane's world, courtesy implied servility. Wearing a smile he had rehearsed for the occasion, nodding toward the only other chair that graced his table, he relaxed and waited for the giant to sit.

Keane knew the giant's name was Nikolai Lukasha, but saw no need to speak the name aloud. This was a business meeting, not a social call, and he was anxious to resolve the problem that had summoned him halfway around the world.

"I'll need a sitrep for the past eight hours," he began, without preliminaries.

Lukasha blinked at him, his eyelids drooping in slow motion. "What is a sitrep?"

Jesus H! he thought. Okay, he'd relax and lead this gomer by the hand, if that was what was needed.

"I've been in and out of airports since your boss called and spoke to mine. I understand you've got a problem on your hands." The smile felt carved into his face. "I'm here to help you, if I can, but first I'll need a sitrep on what's happened since I left the States. Your basic situation report."

Lukasha's homely face remained impassive. He was either hopelessly immune to sarcasm, or else he simply didn't care. "Sitrep," he said again, as if he had to try the word for size once more, before he let it go. "There have been more...how do you say...?"

"Shall we speak Russian?" Keane inquired, the shift in tongues no strain at all.

Lukasha answered him in kind. "There have been two more raids," he said. "The dead now number forty-one."

Keane whistled softly. "All Valerik's men?" he asked.

"Some Germans at the last place," Lukasha said. "Four or five, I think. All people he does business with."

Meaning a bunch of racketeers, drug dealers and whatever else a person would expect to find under a rock. Keane held them in contempt, not for their deeds, but rather for their motives. They were money-grubbing bastards, every one of them. Still, even greed could be a weapon in the proper hands. A patriot could use such men as pawns. They were disposable and easily replaced.

"I don't suppose there's any line yet on the shooters?"

"Everywhere we hear the same," Lukasha answered. "Three men, each time. No clear description, but I think they must be all the same."

"Makes sense. It doesn't give me much to work with, though. I mean, three people in Berlin, it's like your basic needle in a haystack. "I'm starting out with nothing on the shooters, so it's hard to think ahead of them. You follow me? I need a pattern, something, if I'm going to anticipate their moves."

"They seem to strike at random," Lukasha replied. "We have studied maps, but there is nothing to be seen. No pattern, as you say."

Keane sipped his lager, puzzling that one over for a moment, waiting for the light to dawn. There had to be something, if he could—

"They only hit Valerik's places, right? I mean, nothing of Krestyanov's? No German places?"

"Tolya only," the giant said.

"So, the next time they go hunting—and I take for granted there will be a next time—they'll be going after more of Tolya's action." Frowning at a sudden thought, Keane asked, "Has he got anything left standing here in town? They haven't wiped him out already, have they?"

"Still a few things left, I think," Lukasha said. "He doesn't tell us what they are."

"Find out," Keane said, "as soon as possible. We need to narrow the field. We need to concentrate, consolidate. He may not like it, putting all his eggs together, but we need to suck them in, instead of chasing ghosts all over town."

"They may not come," the Russian said.

"You kidding me? These guys have chased Valerik's ass from L.A. to Berlin. You think they'll just give up now and decide to let him walk? If they were quitters, they'd have let him go when he took off for Amsterdam."

"I will request more information."

"Don't request. Demand. Your boss wants this thing taken care of, then we can't afford to coddle Tolya. Anyway, he'd be an idiot to hold back, when you're working overtime to save his ass."

"I will secure the information."

"Better. When we have the details on whatever's left, we'll pick the best spot to defend, clean out the rest and send in every gun available to cover it. How many soldiers can you raise?"

"Valerik has—"

"Not only his," Keane interrupted. "I mean everybody. All for one, and one for all, you dig? You've let this show run too long, as it is. We need to shut it down right here, ASAP."

Lukasha frowned but didn't seem to take offense. After a moment's thought, he said, "We may have fifty guns."

"Does that include your Stasi pals?" Keane asked, rewarded with another clumsy blink. "Hey, don't get sore. The *I* in *CIA* stand for 'intelligence,' remember?"

"That is everyone," Lukasha replied, albeit with a visible reluctance.

"Well, that ought to do the trick," Keane said. "Fifty on three. My kind of odds."

"You will, of course, be there," Lukasha stated, not asking, though his tone conveyed a certain measure of uncertainty.

"You kidding me? Damn right," Keane said. "I wouldn't miss this show for all the bratwurst in Bavaria."

"Figure of speech?" the giant asked.

"You're catching on."

"I go to make things ready, then," Lukasha said, already pushing back his chair.

"You want to let me have a contact number, before you split? I don't intend to hang around this place all night and wait."

Lukasha searched his pockets, came up with a ballpoint pen and spent another moment scratching numerals across the blank side of a paper cocktail napkin. Keane palmed it as the big man rose to leave.

"I'll check in every hour, on the half," he said, tapping the broad face of his Rolex watch with his index finger. "Soon as someone has an address for me, I'll drop by and check it out."

Lukasha nodded, turning toward the exit. Keane's voice stopped the giant in his tracks.

"Just one more thing."

"What?"

"If you've got any pull with the police," he said, "you'll want to have them stay away, all right? No skin off me, but it could look bad for your boy if any uniforms get damage at the party."

"*Da.*" The Russian turned and lumbered through the crowd once more, trusting the Lilliputians in his path to move before he trampled them.

"You bet your sweet ass, *da,*" Keane muttered, picking up his frosty mug as if to toast the giant's exit. "I've got a goddamned freak show, here."

And then he smiled, remembering that he would come out

looking that much better, if his allies seemed inept. The victory would be all his.

FOR THE FIRST TIME in the past six months, since he had been assigned to ferret out the link between Tolya Valerik and the Company, it seemed to Able Deckard that he might be making progress. It was funny, when he thought about it. All the times the CIA had been accused—and rightly so—of breaking laws, avoiding the restrictions of its charter, and the one time when it really mattered, they hadn't gone far enough. If he had simply started killing off Valerik's men six months ago, shooting the bastards down on sight, perhaps he would have wrapped the whole thing up by now, identified and neutralized the danger that was still concealed from him, the jackpot waiting like a booby trap, to blow up in his face.

Or, maybe not.

Deckard couldn't deny he got a rush out of the fighting. Not for killing's sake, but for the sense of *doing* something, after he had wasted so much time without a visible result. Of course, the other way, his life wasn't at risk around the clock, but what the hell. He had a job to do, and it was getting done. Deckard could look out for himself, and he had help from two men who could swing the balance anytime.

He didn't even mind not knowing who they were, exactly. The enigma taunted him, but they were all on the same side, and that was what he really cared about. The thought of having Evan Green and Johnny Gray against him, siding with the enemy, made Deckard feel a little sick inside.

No sweat. They were both on board.

And now, with any luck, he would have something useful to report the next time he spoke to them. Five hundred U.S. dollars had secured an address where a certain Russian was believed to have a rented flat. Deckard had staked it out, and he had been rewarded with a lucky break. No more than twenty minutes on the job, and he had seen Vassily Krestyanov emerge from the apartment house, trailed by a giant of a man who had to be his number two. He trailed the Russians to a popular beer garden, giving them a lead before he followed them inside. They didn't know his face—or shouldn't, anyway—but Krestyanov had been around the cloak-and-dagger game for twenty years or more, and it would be a grave mistake to underestimate his instinct or his skills. As for the hulk who was his shadow, Deckard didn't fancy going one-on-one with someone who could pluck his arms off as if playing with a Barbie doll.

The beer garden was crowded, but he found a place that suited him. It was close enough to watch Krestyanov's booth, but far enough away that neither of the Russians would be likely to detect him watching them. In fact, he found, they hardly looked around at all, Krestyanov busy talking to a bald guy who was seated in the booth beside him, while the hulk worked on his beer. A second, closer look showed Deckard that the third man wasn't simply bald; he had no eyebrows, either, and his jaw was baby-smooth, despite the hour being well advanced.

Compulsive shaver? Deckard wondered, or was the bizarro look a symptom of some ailment? He memorized the face and made a mental note to check with Langley, see if they had anything on file concerning Russian spooks—he'd add the Germans, also, just in case—with alopecia or some similar affliction. Once he got his hands on a computer, he could also whip up alternative faces, giving the bald man a variety of coifs and facial hair.

Although he was a trained lip-reader—handy for those situations where you had to watch your quarry from a distance—Deckard's skill was limited to English, and the heavies in the booth were speaking something else. German or Russian? Deckard couldn't tell. The choice of language might have helped identify their skinhead contact, and he had resolved to risk a walk-by, when he saw that they had wrapped up their business. The giant and Krestyanov left, while the baldman stayed behind and poured himself another brimming mug of beer. Deckard was torn between a sprint to catch the Russians and a need to keep it casual, drawing no special notice to himself, particularly when his targets had at least one ally in the room.

Their car was pulling out when Deckard reached the parking lot. He let it pass, raising a hand to shield his face as if the headlights hurt his eyes, then dashed to reach the Jaguar once Krestyanov's ride was out of sight. Afraid of losing them in Berlin's traffic, Deckard caught a break and spied their car—a small Renault, incongruous with Krestyanov's pet giant at the wheel—stopped at a traffic signal.

Ten minutes later, Deckard knew that they were going home, back to the block of flats where he had picked them up barely an hour earlier. He was surprised, though, when the car stopped out in front and Krestyanov got out, said something to the brutish driver, bending low to face him as he spoke, then went inside alone. The small Renault gave off a yelp of clashing gears, then pulled away.

What now? He could reach out to his companions, give them Krestyanov's address and help them make the hit, but they would be no closer, then, to finding out the object of the exercise. He could remain and watch the flat in case the giant brought someone.

His final option was a gamble, risking loss of contact with Vassily Krestyanov, but Deckard's innate curiosity won out.

He followed the Renault.

Deckard was interested in seeing where the hulk went next.

It was another beer garden, in fact, this one somewhat larger than the first, less trendy, slightly less expensive by its look. Again, Deckard allowed his mark a fair head start, then followed in his wake. One of the bouncers stopped him to collect the cover charge, and Deckard paid in Euros. Damned play money. Every time he handled it, he felt as if he were a kid again, caught up in a game of Monopoly, about to purchase Boardwalk.

Once inside the beer garden, he stepped to one side of the entryway, letting the folks behind him pass, and started looking for the hulk. There was a moment of confusion when he couldn't spot the Russian, Deckard wondering how he could fail to stand out in a crowd. Maybe, if this were a pro basketball convention, but...

The answer came to him at once. The giant had to have found a seat already. Deckard would have to scout the place as unobtrusively as possible, until he found the Russian, no false moves to give himself away.

This was the hard part. Since he couldn't spot his quarry from the doorway, Deckard had to work the room. Bypassing empty booths and tables, he hammed it up a little, frowning to himself, as if he had misplaced a friend, perhaps his date, and was disgruntled at the prospect of a search. The busy waiters left him to it, no one offering to help, which suited Deckard well enough. That way, he didn't have to fabricate descriptions of his mythical companions. He could simply roam the beer garden, pretending to be lost.

So, where the hell was he?

Deckard had scouted one side of the beer garden, was silently debating whether he should check the men's room next, before he searched the other side, when suddenly he saw his man. Slowing, he sidled toward the Russian's table, anxious for a look at his companion. Just a few more steps. If Mr. Big would only lean a little to his left—

He did, and Deckard felt a sudden rush of panic, turning on his heel and walking back in the direction he had come from, praying that he hadn't made the hasty turnaround too obvious, an eye-catcher. The face that he had glimpsed from twenty feet away was seared into his retinas. There could be no mistake.

He knew that face, the name that went along with it.

The Russian's date was Christian Keane.

And Keane was CIA.

12

Bolan was scouting prospects with his brother, rolling east on Ivaliden Strasse, where the great wall once bisected East and West Berlin. Still driving the Volkswagen, with Johnny in the Saab, they kept in touch by cellular phone, staying off the air as much as possible, keeping the conversation cryptic when they spoke. Without a land line, you could never tell exactly who was listening to anything you said. No taps or bugs were necessary, once your voice was broadcast on the airwaves, and no scanner yet devised would tip you that unwelcome ears were listening.

Driving around Berlin made Bolan conscious of how suddenly and radically the world could change. When he was born, throughout his childhood, military service and his lonely war against the Mafia at home, the Wall and all it represented were established facts of life. The world that he grew up in had consisted of two hostile camps, both armed with weapons that could turn the Earth into a lifeless, glowing cinder, drifting aimlessly through space. Every decision made in Washington and Moscow had been predicated on that knowledge, shaded and influenced by the "Balance of Terror."

And then, almost overnight, the Wall was gone. A few months later, the Soviet Union itself had collapsed, a global contest that had spanned three-quarters of a century wiped out, replaced by new uncertainties, new challenges, new threats and rivalries.

Cruising the streets of what had once been East Berlin, Bolan could only wonder if the life he knew and understood was slipping through his fingers. Was it already beyond his reach? Had he and Hal Brognola, his allies at Stony Man, come to a fatal parting of the ways?

Bolan wasn't prepared to write off his friends yet, but neither could he count on them to help him in his present situation. Right now, he trusted Johnny and was leaning strongly toward acceptance of the man he knew as Able Deckard. In their strike against Valerik's drug lab, Deckard had saved Bolan's life *and* Johnny's, while inflicting major damage on the Russian mobster's operation in Berlin. The CIA connection still gave Bolan pause, but if the man had something hidden up his sleeve, it had to be more complex than a simple plan to set them up and knock them over.

It raised some interesting questions, if they threw in with an agent of the CIA against the heavies who were also, somehow, working with the Company. Was Deckard's ''rogue'' scenario correct, or was his operation flying in the face of orders from the brass at Langley? Could *he* be the rogue? And how could Bolan know for sure without reliable intelligence from Stony Man?

For now, he was prepared to tough it out, take Deckard at face value, while remaining on alert for an eleventh-hour double cross. As far as dealing with the Company itself, or any faction of it that was cozy with Valerik's Family and-or the former KGB, Bolan would jump off that cliff when he reached it.

The target he was scouting at the moment was another warehouse, fronting on a river near the point where Rathausstrasse crossed an old but sturdy-looking bridge. So much of what had once been East Berlin was run-down, compared to structures in the western sector, that he had a sense of driving through a slum, where everything except official buildings and a few shops catering to leaders of the ruling party showed signs of a terminal neglect.

So much for communism's glorious Utopia.

The warehouse wore a bland facade like any other in the district—any other in the world, for that matter. How many times had Bolan cracked a target that appeared substantially the same, innocuous as far as any passersby could tell, but sheltering a secret sin behind plain walls?

The joint in question was supposed to be a chop shop, with a twist. As Able Deckard ran it down, it served the normal function of remodeling or stripping stolen cars, but also "customized" legitimate vehicles bound for shipment overseas, equipping them with secret hidey-holes where anything from heroin to stolen gems could be concealed—and hopefully avoid the watchful eyes of customs on arrival in Great Britain, Canada or the United States. Destruction of the plant itself, assuming they could pull it off, would set Tolya Valerik back a hefty piece of change. Whatever contraband they managed to destroy along the way would just be icing on the cake.

The cellular phone chirped, and Bolan picked it up before it could repeat the shrill, insectile sound. *"Ja."*

"Mein brüder." My brother. He could picture Johnny grinning at him, putting on the heavy accent, with a dash of Hollywood.

"What's up?"

"I'm checking out that other thing we talked about," Johnny said, an oblique reference to their secondary target, an exclusive sporting house on Hohenzollern Damm.

"So, how's it look?" Bolan asked.

"If you ask me, they could use some more security," the kid replied. "Of course, I can't say what it's like inside."

"They're working, though?"

"Affirmative. From what I've seen, I'd estimate a couple dozen customers. It could be more."

Civilians, that would be. It didn't rule out the mission, but Bolan would prefer a target where he didn't have to deal with noncombatants in the line of fire.

"This other deal looks clean," Bolan said. "Should be an easy in-and-out."

"Suits me," his brother said. "I'll meet you there. Twenty minutes."

"I'll see you then."

Bolan had barely hung up, when the phone produced another chirping sound. He hesitated, frowning as he picked it up again.

"*Ja?*"

"It's me," Able Deckard said, sounding grim.

"Okay."

"We need to meet ASAP," the man from Langley stated.

"Okay," the Executioner replied. "I'm at that place we talked about, the condo with the river view. I'll keep an eye out if you want to drop on by."

"Are you alone?" Deckard asked.

Bolan felt the short hairs stirring on his nape.

"We split the list to speed things up," he said, and let it go at that. The question made him curious, and it was only baby steps from curious to paranoid.

"I think all of us need to talk," Deckard said. "No point going through the story twice."

"How about a preview?" Bolan asked. "They've always been my favorite part of going to the movies."

"You want a trailer, fine. How's this—guy trails his girlfriend to a bar, thinking she may hook up with someone else behind his back. When he walks in, it turns out that she's meeting with an old friend from his graduating class. You like that story line?"

"I'll see you back at the hotel," Bolan said, breaking the connection, mashing down a button with his thumb to speed dial Johnny's cellular phone.

"Yeah?"

"Our buddy just checked in," Bolan replied. "He's got something for us, but he wants to meet at the hotel."

"You kidding me?" Johnny answered. "I'm still scouting—"

"This could be important," Bolan interrupted him. "It seems our hosts have company from home."

Johnny was silent for a moment, muffled street sounds in the background. When he spoke again, he asked, "You think it's straight?"

"One way to check it out."

"Okay." Reluctantly. "I'll see you there in ten, maybe fifteen."

"Stay frosty," Bolan said, and cut the link before his brother could reply.

His old misgivings about Able Deckard, lately sublimated, suddenly came back to haunt him. Bolan told himself the obvious—that Deckard wouldn't tip him off if he were scheming with a gang of spooks fresh off the latest flight from Washington, but that didn't go far toward putting Bolan's mind at ease. Any appearance of the CIA in Berlin, at the moment, had to be bad news for Bolan, Johnny and their move against Valerik. He could sugarcoat it until doomsday, but the basic fact remained: some portion of the Company, whether official or a group of rogues, was backing Valerik's play with members of the former KGB. The bad news was that he still had no idea of what Valerik's plan entailed, and each soldier added to the opposition force increased the likelihood that he—the Executioner—would be rubbed out, along with Johnny and Suzanne, before he answered that most basic question.

Still, he knew there was no way he could simply blow off Able Deckard's warning—not if he intended to survive. If Deckard said that he had spotted men from Langley in Berlin, the fact required investigation, at the very least. As far as a response…well, that would have to wait for Bolan's personal analysis of the details. Even assuming Deckard chose to go against his fellow spooks, Bolan would want to hear his story face-to-face, see how he looked and acted in the flesh, before he chose a course of action for himself.

Reluctantly, he terminated his surveillance of the warehouse, starting back toward the hotel where Suzanne King was housed. It had already crossed his mind that Deckard—or his cronies—could have set an ambush up at the hotel, but what would be the point when he could just as easily have let them die in the assault against Valerik's drug lab?

No.

It made no sense, and Bolan was prepared to trust Deckard that far, at least. But if there was a trap at the hotel, if there was anything amiss that linked in any way to Deckard's urgent summons, he would pay.

In blood.

SOMETIMES MANFRED Berghoff surprised himself. It was a part of life—and business, certainly—that he should boast of his achievements and abilities. In thirteen years as an inspector, counterspy and finally interrogator for the Stasi—East Germany's dreaded and murderous secret police, an echo of the older, larger KGB—Berghoff had scored his share of triumphs, granted. He had unmasked Western agents in Berlin, participated in their capture or elimination, helped to break those who survived the rigors of arrest, and made damned sure his name was represented in as many files as possible, with flattering descriptions of his work.

These days, of course, when everything had changed, "achievements" from the old regime were often looked upon as crimes. There was no movement, yet, to prosecute the Stasi agents who had been identified—so damned careless to not double-check that the files had all been burned before the

Wall came down—but Berghoff was perpetually on alert for any subtle changes in the temper of the times.

Meanwhile, he had a reputation as a man who got things done. And part of that outstanding reputation was a skein of truths, half-truths and outright lies that he had woven for himself.

Berghoff was good, of course, but sometimes when he really scored against the odds, he felt an unexpected thrill of pride, as if the game were new again, compelled to prove his value in a world of canny veterans.

It should have taken him a long, long time to trace the girl, assuming he was able to discover her at all. Berlin was one of modern Europe's major cities, with a full-time population rapidly approaching 3.4 million residents. It has more than a hundred advertised hotels, not counting B & B's, apartment houses, youth hostels and rooms for let in private homes. Tourism was a major source of income in the German capital, and English-speaking businessmen were everywhere, ubiquitous. Unless a visitor was Asian, black or opted to immolate himself outside the Philharmonic Hall at rush hour, the chances were that he—or she—would pass unnoticed in Berlin.

But he got lucky. He had a grainy photograph, faxed from America and poorly duplicated at a local studio, which he distributed among his troops. Two of them got lucky at the fourth hotel they tried.

The concierge was hesitant at first, admitting only that the fuzzy black-and-white bore ''some resemblance'' to a guest who had recently arrived. Berghoff's employees mixed a touch of bribery with a bit of intimidation to produce a more assertive judgment. Cash in hand persuaded their informant that the woman in the photo was indeed the occupant of room 963, while a description of the methods they would use— sans anesthetic—to remove that hand now holding the cash, if he was wrong, assured them that he wasn't simply lying for the money.

Theoretically, at least.

There would be more than grubby hands cut off if this turned out to be a wild-goose chase, but Berghoff was an optimist at heart. He saw a glass half-full, whenever possible, and smashed it with a sledgehammer if circumstances proved him wrong.

The trick now, as he saw it, was to take his quarry by surprise. The worst-case scenario had Berghoff's targets spooked and bailing out ahead of him, so that he had to start the hunt from scratch. Another script—his favorite—had all of them on hand when he arrived, resisting to the death.

Whatever happened, Berghoff knew how fortunate he was to score a hit this early in his search, and he was determined not to blow it if it was within his power to succeed. Vassily Krestyanov still had influence with important men in Moscow. He could help Berghoff advance, make him a wealthy man—or he could simply pull the plug, have the German taken out one day, when Berghoff least expected it, depending on the outcome of the search.

Berghoff didn't inform Krestyanov that the woman had been located. If she slipped through his hands, or if the concierge had spoken out of greed and wishful thinking, Berghoff could erase the incident, proceed with his search of the capital as if there had been no distraction early on.

And best of all, he wouldn't come off looking like a hopeless idiot.

Berghoff took thirteen soldiers with him, just in case. For all their fearsome reputation, he didn't believe that any three Americans, if truly taken by surprise, could shoot their way out of the trap he had in mind. Assuming they were present and accounted for, Berghoff didn't believe his quarry would be able to escape their rooms. In any case, he would have bet his life that they couldn't slip out of the hotel.

When they arrived at the hotel, three carloads of them, automatic weapons barely hidden under tailored jackets, Berghoff wasted no time cornering the concierge, breathing down his sweaty neck until the man had produced a fairly detailed sketch of the fourth floor. Sadly, the concierge had no idea if the Americans were presently upstairs. Their three rooms had been cleaned that morning, but the best part of twelve hours had elapsed since then, and nothing would be gained by questioning the housekeepers. For all he knew, the Yanks could be out on the town, or tucked up in their cozy beds, in any combination that their hearts desired.

Berghoff decided he couldn't afford to wait. Delay was often fatal, and he wouldn't have it said by Krestyanov that he had wasted precious time, when moving with dispatch could have resulted in his quarry being tagged and bagged.

"Alive if possible," he told his men once more, when they had been divided into four-man teams, had palmed their passkeys, and were ready for the long jog up the service stairs to the ninth floor. Manfred Berghoff himself would lead the party that assaulted room 963.

There were no other guests in evidence when they arrived on nine, though Berghoff could hear televisions playing from behind a number of the doors.

Berghoff dispatched his teams to 961 and 919, the latter room some distance down the hall. He pondered the significance of placement for a moment, then dismissed it as irrelevant, pressing an ear against the door of room 963 to see if he could pick up any noise from inside.

Nothing.

He nodded to Joachim, who held the passkey, standing back to let the others soak up any gunfire from the room, in case their targets were already on alert. The Walther P-1 pistol in his hand was the same weapon he had carried every day when he was working for the Stasi, in the good old days when he was still respected, not required to lie about his past.

The days that Krestyanov assured him would be coming back, before much longer—only better than before.

The passkey was a perfect fit, and Berghoff let his shooters lead the way, closing the door behind him as he stepped into the room. He found the sleeping quarters empty, with his men clustered around the bathroom door. It was ajar and spilling light, the sound of rushing water indicating that someone was in the shower.

Berghoff pushed past the others, through the bathroom door, noting the plastic shower curtain as it rippled from the sudden draft. A woman's sultry voice said, "Johnny, I'm so glad you're back. Why don't you get in here and let me wash your—"

"Madam," Berghoff interrupted her in English, secretly delighted with the gasp his unfamiliar voice elicited, "I think it preferable if you, perhaps, come out."

DRIVING NORTH along Bundes Allee, toward the hotel and Suzanne, Johnny tried to imagine what was so important that they had to scrub a scouting mission just to meet with Deckard. What was wrong with Deckard that he couldn't choose a mutually convenient midway point, instead of reeling in Johnny and his brother like children being summoned home for dinner of an evening?

He felt slightly churlish, even thinking in that vein, after the man had saved his life, but that was combat. He was grateful, obviously, for the CIA man's intercession when Valerik's gunner was about to take him out, but Deckard had preserved his life so Johnny could go on to fight another day. In order for him to fulfill that destiny, he had to do the groundwork, scout the territory, check out his adversaries with any means at his disposal.

And the urgent call from Able Deckard, relayed through his brother, was preventing him from doing that.

Chill out, he told himself, and tried to concentrate on driving, rather than the irritation that had gripped him when he got the summons to return and meet with Deckard. There was good news, in addition to the interruption, since a stop at the hotel meant he would get to see Suzanne, might even find an opportunity to be alone with her, although—

"Chill out!"

This time he spoke the words aloud, disturbed at how the shift in focus had immediately changed his attitude from irritation over Deckard's interruption of his scouting, to a warm-and-fuzzy feeling at the prospect of a little R & R. He was professional enough to recognize the weakness in himself, and knew that he would have to guard against it every moment from now on, until such time as any danger from Tolya Valerik and his allies had been finally eliminated.

Johnny would never qualify as a defeatist, and he wasn't frightened of Valerik's gangland "Family." With his brother's help, he had already chased the bastards from Los Angeles, clean out of the United States and on to Europe. They were tough enough in ordinary circumstances, and he knew the kind of panic Russian mobsters threw into unarmed civilians, especially their own conditioned countrymen, but frankly, Johnny hadn't been impressed by their endurance under fire, so far.

What troubled him—no, make that *worried* him—was the idea of taking out Valerik and his hardmen, only to become embroiled in endless conflict with the CIA. The notion took him back to his brother's days as a fugitive from justice, during Johnny's adolescence, when his brother's face was found on Wanted posters, broadcast on the television network news between reports of summit meetings in the Middle East and hurricanes in the Caribbean. It was beyond him how Mack had survived those years in exile, hunted by the cops *and* by the robbers simultaneously, both sides operating under orders that required them to shoot first and save their questions for a rainy day.

Part of the trick to his brother's survival, Johnny knew, had been the covert help he had received from Hal Brognola, even though it jeopardized the Fed's career, his very liberty. There would be none of that this time around, he understood, for either member of the Bolan family. If the brothers managed to survive the next few hours or days, if they were driven underground, he reckoned that they would be on their own.

Johnny had sampled loneliness, and then some, in his younger days, but even at the worst of it—his parents and his sister dead, his brother in the wind, a hunted felon—there had always been a sense of someone standing on the sidelines, sometimes hidden in the shadows, looking out for him. The cops were there, of course, if only to complain about how Congress and the courts had tied their hands. Child Welfare got involved, and while he knew the social workers were sincere, Johnny had learned the four most terrifying words a bureaucrat can ever say: "I'm here to help." At last, there had been Val Querente and John Gray, a Fed who did help, not by quoting rules and regulations, but by simply opening his heart.

Johnny bypassed the hotel's valet and parked the Saab himself. When he was halfway to the glass revolving doors, he saw the VW Passat enter the parking lot and doubled back to meet his brother at the car. There was no sign yet of Able Deckard or his flashy Jaguar.

"I thought he'd beat us here," Johnny said.

His brother responded with a shrug. "He didn't say where he was coming from."

"So, what's the deal with meeting here? I understand about not talking on the air, but jeez!"

Another shrug. "I told you everything the man told me."

Johnny checked out the hotel lobby as they entered, just in case, and felt his brother doing likewise. Other than a balding clerk behind the registration desk and one man lounging on a sofa, paging through a newspaper, they had the whole place to themselves. No Deckard, no apparent ambush.

Yet.

"You want the elevator or the stairs?" Johnny asked.

"Better make it stairs."

There was no need for him to add the *just in case* part. It was understood. If Deckard's summons was some kind of trap, and they hadn't been hit downstairs, it stood to reason that the shooters would be waiting for them up on nine. With elevators, you were trapped inside a metal box, nowhere to go if someone started shooting when the door slid open. On the service stairs, at least, they would have some degree of combat stretch.

It was a hike, though. Nine floors up meant eighteen flights of stairs, their footsteps scraping with an echo in the stairwell, even though they tried to keep it down. A welcoming committee, on the other hand, would be in place already, standing silently and waiting, with their weapons cocked and locked.

On five, Johnny took time to lean across the railing, peering up the stairwell, as if he expected to see faces staring down at him with Bad Guy tattooed on their foreheads.

"What?" his brother asked.

"Nothing. Forget it."

Johnny's jacket was unbuttoned, had been since he put it on that morning. Ever conscious of the pistol slung beneath his arm, he hooked a thumb behind his belt buckle, hoping to shave another heartbeat off his draw if shooting was required.

No one had braced them by the time they got to nine, and it was Johnny's turn to be first through the door. It was a fire door, solid steel, no window for a look-through, so he had to take his chances, hoping that its bulk would offer some protection if a shooter in the hallway opened up.

The hallway was deserted, and he moved along toward

room 963, his brother close behind him now. A pause to look and listen at the room they shared next door, 961, but there were no lights showing, and he heard no sounds. At Suzanne's door, he hesitated, stiffened at the faint sound of a male voice speaking German, then relaxed as background music and a laugh track told him that she had the television on.

He knocked, got no response and tried again. Three times, in fact. He saw his brother frowning, knew the grim expression had to be mirrored on his own face. If Suzanne heard them—

"Do you have a key?" Bolan asked, interrupting the thought.

He nodded, felt the warm blush in his cheeks, despite the fact that his brother knew all about him and Suzanne.

The "key" was actually a plastic card. When Johnny slid his card into the slot, he felt the door move, swinging slowly inward.

The automatic pistol seemed to fill his hand without a conscious thought. He called out Suzanne's name repeatedly, as he was moving through the empty suite of rooms, but all he got in answer was another round of laughter from the television. Doubling back to catch it, Johnny slapped the power button, switching off the TV.

"She's gone," he said, as if his brother were a blind man. In the bathroom, lying rumpled on the floor, he found a towel still damp from Suzanne's body. There was water dripping lightly in the shower, condensation slowly fading on the mirror opposite.

"Out here," Bolan said, and Johnny joined him in the main room, found him standing by the bed. There was a piece of paper in his brother's hand, which Johnny recognized as hotel stationery.

The note was printed in block letters, by a hand that seldom wrote in English. It was perfectly succinct: "Grunewald. Midnight."

A noise behind them, in the doorway, brought both guns around to frame a target Johnny had forgotten in his sudden rush of anguish.

Able Deckard raised his empty hands and said, "Hey, guys. Did I miss something?"

13

There was a certain trick to writing ransom notes. You shouldn't say too little, or too much. Whenever possible, a pro will let the crime scene tell its story, do most of his talking for him. Johnny knew, therefore, that he was dealing with a pro.

The note in Suzanne's room had told him where to go—Grunewald, a massive park in the southwestern quarter of Berlin—and when to be there.

Because the Grunewald was so large and Johnny had been given no coordinates, he took for granted that the men he was supposed to meet would make a point of finding him. He also took for granted that they meant to kill him, kill whoever might accompany him and then eliminate Suzanne. Thus, as they had to have worked it out beforehand, they would finally be rid of those who had harassed Tolya Valerik and his soldiers for the past two weeks.

Unfortunately for the plotters, they were bound to fail, no matter how the Grunewald ambush finally played out.

For Johnny would be coming to the meeting alone.

His brother had opposed the move initially, but after they had talked it over, it was clear that any hope of wrapping up the action in Berlin relied on a division of their forces—taking out the Hydra's several heads at once, if possible.

Suzanne's abduction was a setup, plain and simple. Her kidnappers hoped to draw their quarry in, catch all of them together in the Grunewald and annihilate them where they stood. It was a game they had to have played before, with other pawns, but Johnny was about to change the rules.

What the kidnappers didn't know, or hadn't stopped to think, was that the game had moved light-years beyond Suzanne and Billy King. His personal feelings aside, Johnny understood that his and Mack's mission—destroying the Russian Mob's connection to the CIA—had to take priority over Suzanne's safe recovery. He also knew, from grim experience, that it was fifty-fifty she had already been killed. The men behind the ambush wouldn't leave her corpse at the hotel, and thus defeat their plan, but they might very well have decided she was expendable once they had cleared the scene.

Johnny knew his visit to the Grunewald might be wasted effort, playing hide-and-seek with Death to no result. He also understood that even if Suzanne was still alive, he couldn't sacrifice the mission to protect her.

But he could raise holy hell with those responsible for her abduction while he had the chance.

The Grunewald was primarily for strollers, much like New York's Central Park. A few roads penetrated the greenery, but since no destination had been specified by those he was supposed to meet, he saw no point in cruising aimlessly around the park. It made more sense for him to leave the Saab, start walking, and be ready when the trap was sprung. With any luck at all, he might surprise the shooters, throw them just a little bit off balance, maybe place *them* at a handicap.

He found a public parking lot, deserted now, and left the Saab. It had no theft alarm installed, but Johnny didn't care. Car thieves were far down the list of his priorities, right now. As for the risk of meeting muggers in the Grunewald, Johnny almost wished he would.

It could have been good exercise, a warm-up for the main event.

He wore his pistol, the CZ-75, beneath his left arm, while the Uzi submachine gun hung below his right, its sling rigged out of strips that he had cut from a bath towel at the hotel. Spare magazines for both guns were distributed as evenly as possible in Johnny's pockets, to prevent unnecessary noise and help relieve him from a sense of being lopsided. All told, he carried seventy-five rounds for the pistol and 160 for the SMG. It sounded like a lot, but in the heat of battle, ammunition had a way of literally going up in smoke.

The night was cool, and he was grateful for the trench coat as protection from the breeze, as much as for concealment of his weapons. Even with the coat on and a turtleneck beneath it, he could still feel goose bumps rising on his back and arms.

Just nerves, he thought, and kept on walking, his hands inside the pockets of his coat. Johnny had slit the right-hand pocket with a knife, so he could reach the Uzi without opening the trench coat, and he had his fingers wrapped around the pistol grip, drawing substantial comfort from the weapon's solid weight against his side.

While Johnny roamed the Grunewald, waiting for the fireworks to begin, his brother would be taking on Tolya Valerik. Able Deckard would be squaring off with the assorted spooks whom he had recognized. The news of yet another CIA man in Berlin, meeting with former agents of the KGB, had clearly shaken Deckard, but he had seemed to think that it would help him nail the rogues at Langley.

If they were rogues.

If his whole damned story wasn't smoke and mirrors, something cooked up by the enemy to sidetrack Bolan and Johnny.

Trudging through the darkness, listening for any sounds that would betray pursuers or alert him to an ambush up ahead, Johnny considered how he should dispose of Deckard if, in spite of everything, the guy turned out to be a rat.

It would depend, he finally decided, on how Suzanne fared this night. If she was killed or seriously injured, and he learned that Deckard had some part in it, Johnny would make his death as slow and painful as the time and opportunity permitted. If he managed to retrieve her from her captors, and they somehow both survived the night, then Johnny might be merciful. A quick, clean kill would be enough.

He recognized the symptoms of distraction, snapped his mind back to the present as he worked his way deeper into the park. A false step here and now could end both his life and Suzanne's. If she was still alive, he meant to keep her that way.

He was focused on the path ahead when suddenly a voice addressed him from the darkness. "You may stop there."

DECKARD HAD squeezed one of his sources for an address on Valerik's normal hideout in Berlin, but he wasn't prepared to guarantee the Russian would be waiting there for Bolan to arrive.

"You want me to," the man from Langley had declared, "I'll tag along and keep you company. It could get hairy, if he's calling in the troops."

Bolan had turned down the offer for three reasons. First, having accepted Johnny's plan for a division of their forces, he wasn't about to give himself an edge his brother lacked. Second, he knew that for the plan to work, each member of the team had to do his part, take out the separate targets as assigned. And finally, in spite of everything, there was the niggling remnant of a doubt in Bolan's mind that Deckard couldn't be trusted all the way.

If anything went wrong, and Deckard showed up uninvited, it would mean that he was fighting for the other side, and Bolan wouldn't need to hesitate before he struck.

Valerik's safehouse was a country villa, situated several miles north of Berlin. To get there, Bolan drove out Prenzlauer Allee until the city lights began to dwindle, then turned off onto a narrow country lane. The place he sought wasn't a mansion, but it was supposed to be secure, with troops in residence, their number presently unknown.

As if it mattered.

Bolan was prepared to face the odds, whatever they might be, and see his mission through. Valerik was his handle on the whole damned thing, though he no longer seemed to be the central figure. If they had a chance to talk, it would be helpful, but he wasn't counting on it. In any case, no matter what went down, regardless of the measures he had taken to protect himself, Tolya Valerik had to go.

Player or pawn, the Russian *mafioso* obviously had something that made him valuable to past and present spooks from both sides of the late cold war. And from the effort they had made, the blood that they had spilled trying to cover up their tracks, Bolan felt confident in guessing they planned to turn up the heat very soon.

It troubled him, not knowing what the heavies had in mind, when he had come so far and put in so much time. It would be better if he knew the detailed workings of their plan, but Bolan reckoned it might not be absolutely necessary. Once you knew the players, if you took them out, the game was over, and the table stakes became irrelevant. He didn't favor flying blind, but if the choice came down to that or standing still, then he would close his eyes and hang on for dear life.

Hiking through darkness, from the point where he had left the Volkswagen, Bolan carried the Galil assault rifle, stock folded, with a 50-round box magazine in place. He wore the second Uzi slung across his back, with the Beretta Model 92 and spare mags in a fast-draw shoulder rig. His face and hands were darkened to avoid reflecting moonlight as he crossed the open fields, homing on lights that marked his target's hideaway.

Ten minutes more brought him to the perimeter. There was

no fence or wall around the property, but he spent several moments checking for security devices small enough to pass unnoticed in the night. There seemed to be no motion sensors, infrared detectors or the like, but he couldn't rule out long-distance watchers, either manning Starlite scopes or sitting at a monitor inside the villa, letting cameras scan the grounds.

If there were lookouts and they had him spotted, Bolan reckoned there was nothing he could do about it now. Retreating would be dangerous, perhaps more so than pushing on. If he was going to risk death in any case, he might as well continue and engage his enemies.

He met the first sentry a hundred yards from the house, patrolling in the shadow of a one-time barn that had apparently become an oversized garage. The hardman had a submachine gun, one of the German MP-Ks, but he never got a chance to use it. Bolan, stepping from the darkness, fired the Galil. The gunman staggered, slumped against the east wall of the barn and was supported there until a roundhouse kick lashed out and broke his neck.

It was another moment's work for Bolan to secure the corpse, dragging it out of sight behind the barn-garage. He left the MP-K with its late owner, but he pulled the 32-round magazine and pitched it far into the darkness, out of sight.

The Executioner moved on, in search of other prey.

SUZANNE KING worked her lips against the duct tape covering her mouth, tried pushing with her tongue, but the reward for all her pains was simply that: more pain. Her lips and cheeks felt chapped and raw, as if she had been standing out in Arctic winds for hours.

And still, she couldn't speak, could utter no more than a muffled grunting sound.

If she did even that much, Suzanne had discovered, she would be rewarded with still greater pain. Her wrists were pinned behind her back, secured by handcuffs, and the man assigned to manage her kept one hand on the chain between the cuffs, prepared to wrench her arms back with an agonizing twist if Suzanne disobeyed her orders to be still. The bastard only had to do it once—"for practice," as he said— before she got the point.

At first, when she was cornered by these strangers in her hotel suite, Suzanne had thought they meant to kill her on the spot. Later, while driving through the darkened streets, she kept expecting one of them to slash her throat or shoot her in the head, then pitch her body from the car. It wasn't until they reached the park that Suzanne realized why she was still alive.

They needed bait.

If she had known that in advance, when they were back at the hotel, she could have made things difficult, forced them to shoot her and thereby derailed their plans. Her eyes stung with the bitter tears of shame and failure, knowing that her own survival for a few more minutes could result in Johnny Gray or Mike Belasko being killed.

Suzanne wished they would simply leave her to the kidnappers, and beat the ambush that way, but she knew Johnny, at least, would never let her go without a fight. He would have risked his life to save hers, even if they weren't involved, and knowing he would come for her compounded her instinctive sense of guilt.

It was her goddamned fault, she told herself. All of it.

Off to Suzanne's left, one of her captors muttered something, speaking German. Though she didn't understand a word of it, she felt the change in attitude among the men surrounding her, and felt her private watchdog grip the chain between her cuffs tighter, putting just a hint of pressure on her shoulder joints. In case the threat of simple pain wasn't enough, he also jammed what Suzanne took to be the muzzle of a gun against her ribs.

There was someone coming.

Certain of it, even as the thought took form, she hoped it would be some Berliner on a nightly stroll—walking a dog, perhaps, or even looking for a woman he could flash. She prayed that it wouldn't be anyone she knew, no brave man risking life and limb on vain attempts to save her, when she was already doomed.

Too late.

From the excitement of her keepers, Suzanne knew they had a live one, but she also sensed a certain disappointment when their leader—a German who was completely hairless—hissed something to his cronies, silencing the rest of them.

What was it? she wondered. Had something gone wrong?

A moment later, dragged from her position to a better vantage point, Suzanne could see the problem for herself. One man was moving toward them through the darkness, on his own. Just one. The plot to make it a clean sweep was going down in flames.

And Suzanne didn't need to see the lone man's face. If only one of them had come for her, she knew it would be Johnny. Even if it meant defying Deckard and Belasko, he would make the effort on his own. For her.

She was about to make her move, and screw the gun that gouged her ribs, when the German beat her to it, calling out to Johnny in his stilted English, "You may stop there."

The figure stopped in shadow, his face invisible, but Suzanne didn't need to see his face. She recognized the body, clothed or naked. She was thoroughly conversant with the way he moved.

The German barked an order, and her escort shoved Suzanne in front of him, into the open. At the same time, she could feel the pistol shift, lose contact, angling toward the spot where Johnny stood.

"You see, my word is good," the German said, with a gloating tone that made her long to find some heavy object, anything at all, and smash his hairless face. "Frankly, I was expecting more than one of you."

"The others couldn't make it," Johnny said. "They both had dates."

"Ah, well," the German replied, "then I'm afraid that you must do."

Suzanne got ready for the pain, kicked backward with her right foot, driving hard against her escort's shin, and threw herself against him as all hell broke loose.

"THIS REALLY sucks," Deckard muttered to the night as he prepared to make another head count of his enemies.

The guards on Krestyanov were new. The last time he had passed this way, watching Krestyanov step out of the car before he trailed the hulking giant to his meet with Christian Keane, there had been no sentries in evidence. Now, there were two on the stoop, another pair parked in a car downrange, away to Deckard's left, and someone up in what he took for Krestyanov's fourth-floor apartment had begun to check the street below at seven-minute intervals.

Five men, at least, and maybe more in back if he could get there to check it out.

Deckard was less concerned with who the soldiers were than why they had appeared so suddenly to stand guard over Krestyanov. It could be that the colonel had a nervous streak, with all the trouble lately in Berlin, but Deckard didn't think so. If the shooters were Krestyanov's, or if he had seen fit to request them when the killing started, the CIA agent would have seen them on his first two visits earlier that night.

Which meant there had to be something special going on.

There was that business with the girl, of course. Deckard was glad to be relieved of that chore, but he wasn't sure of the connection, told himself it didn't quite make sense. If Valerik's people were expecting major fireworks at the

Grunewald swap, they should be sending people over there, instead of dumping them on Krestyanov.

Or did these shooters represent another faction joining in the game?

Could they be CIA?

He weighed the Ingram MAC-10 in his hand and double-checked the Glock, securely nestled in its shoulder holster. Deckard was as ready as he'd ever be, but challenging four shooters on the sidewalk, while his target watched and laughed at him from four floors up, would be idiotic.

He had to get around in back—or try, at least—and see if there was some way to get in without a major firefight in the middle of the street.

That meant retreating through the alley that concealed him, plus a hike around the block, but Deckard used the time to think about the move he was about to make. If Christian Keane was putting gunners on the street to cover someone like Vassily Krestyanov, there had to be a reason. Running with the notion, Deckard wondered if his own immediate superiors had dropped a stitch or missed a memo. Maybe there were wires crossed, back at Langley, and the whole damned thing was a mistake. For all that Deckard knew, he could be psyching up to kill men who were really on his side.

Bullshit!

No one made a mistake like that, not even in the cloak-and-dagger world where fuck-ups were routine and often deadly. Krestyanov had dealings with Valerik—and apparently with Christian Keane, as well. Keane had to be the pipeline back to Langley, where he worked directly under...

"Christ!"

And there were only two things he could do, right now: bail and be a healthy coward, or proceed and see what hit the fan.

Another alley ran behind Krestyanov's building. Deckard

saw what seemed to be a solitary figure halfway down, approximately where the back door ought to be, if his perspective wasn't skewed.

Last chance, he told himself. He could forget the whole damned thing and walk on by.

Deckard turned into the alley, walking with his head down, hoping that the shooter didn't have a walkie-talkie, but figuring he had to. How else could he get orders, stay in contact with his people on the street?

The CIA agent was down to praying that it wouldn't be someone he knew, had talked to, seen around the halls or in the cafeteria at Langley, no one he had worked with on some other case. He wasn't altogether sure that he could kill a man with whom he had shared coffee. He was thinking through it, wondering what he should say, if anything, before he pulled the trigger, but the voice he heard came from outside his head.

And it was speaking German.

What the hell…?

Relief may have been written on his face as Deckard glanced up toward the shooter, squinting, as if darkness somehow made it difficult for him to hear. He saw the lookout had a headset on, the small mike on a curved arm, out in front, and Deckard knew that he was out of time.

He raised the Ingram, killed the German where he stood and stepped across his body, toward the back door of the house.

"WE SHOULD HAVE gone home yesterday." Vassily Krestyanov didn't sound bitter when he spoke, but there was weariness and something very much like resignation in his voice.

"We still have time," Nikolai Lukasha said. He was busy reassembling an AKSU automatic rifle, the stubby weapon resembling a toy in his oversized hands.

"I hope that won't be necessary," Krestyanov remarked.

"A small precaution, like the guards."

Krestyanov had reluctantly allowed Manfred Berghoff to send a team of bodyguards to watch for trouble when it had become apparent that the violence in Berlin was escalating. So far, all the targets had been Valerik's men, but that could change at any moment if the faceless enemy found out Valerik's link to Krestyanov. His flight to Moscow would be taking off at 9:00 a.m., but in the meantime, it was better to be paranoid than dead.

Six guards, including one who occupied Krestyanov's sitting room, checking the window constantly and still, Krestyanov didn't feel secure. Berlin had soured for him, and he had begun to wonder if perhaps the scheme he had devised with so much loving care was doomed to fail.

The news from Noble Pruett, carried by his intermediary, hadn't been encouraging. The CIA—or Pruett's part of it, at least—had no idea who was responsible for the attacks on Valerik, other than to point a finger at the woman, Suzanne King, and the nonentity she had employed to find her missing brother. It was perfectly ridiculous and typically American, this fantasy of two civilians blazing a trail of death across two continents, eluding or annihilating cadres of professional assassins. If they filmed the story, Krestyanov supposed Tom Cruise would play the hero's role and ride into the sunset with his lover in the final reel.

"Pathetic horseshit!"

"Sir?"

Krestyanov blinked, surprised to find that he had spoken. Lukasha was staring at him quizzically, the AKSU resting on his bony knees.

"It's nothing, Nikolai," Krestyanov answered. "Or, possibly, I'm going mad."

"It's being cooped up in this place," Lukasha said, fanning the air with one huge hand to indicate the small apartment. "We should go wait at the airport, maybe have some dinner on the way. If we're not sleeping, what's the difference? At the airport, they have breathing room.''

"You're right, of course," Krestyanov said.

They were already packed, nothing to do but have the watchdogs load their luggage in the car and take them to the airport. They would be forced to leave their weapons in the car, but that wasn't a problem. German airports were well known for their security.

"We're going, then?" Lukasha asked.

"Why not?"

"Thank God!" The giant rose and nodded toward the sitting room. "I'll have the boy call up a couple of his friends to get the bags."

The bodyguard wasn't amused. He came in red faced, frowning mightily. "I have my orders, sir," he said.

"Your orders have been changed," Krestyanov said.

"I need to ask Berghoff."

"Then, by all means, ask him. Do your duty." Pointing toward the nightstand, Krestyanov informed him, "There's the telephone."

"I was instructed not to bother him," the soldier said, looking embarrassed now.

"You're in a quandary, then," Krestyanov replied. "To ask, or not to ask? I must advise you that my friend and I are leaving momentarily, whether you choose to come along or not. Myself, I think Berghoff may be disappointed in you if you let us make our journey to the airport all alone."

The soldier realized that he was cornered. There could be no reasoning with Russians, after all. At last, however grudgingly, he nodded acquiescence.

"As you say, sir. Let me call down for help."

Five minutes later, they were set to go, two German shooters carrying the luggage, while Krestyanov took his own briefcase and Lukasha brought up the rear, the AKSU hidden underneath his long black coat. It felt good to be moving, even if their destination of the moment was another holding pen, another wait. At least they would be that much closer to escaping from Berlin.

The simple act of leaving his apartment seemed to liberate Vassily Krestyanov. He felt an almost childish urge to smile as they were trooping toward the elevator. Lukasha reached out to push the button for the lobby, and they waited, listening as mighty cables hummed and rattled in the elevator shaft.

What Krestyanov did not hear was the muffled opening and closing of a nearby door that granted access to the service stairs. It was a rather subtle movement, flickering at the very edge of his peripheral vision, which alerted Krestyanov to peril.

Turning to his left, he saw a stranger standing in the middle of the hallway, leveling some kind of automatic weapon with a bulky sound suppressor attached.

"I'm glad you're packed," the stranger said in English, smiling as he spoke, "because it's checkout time."

14

The first guard had been careless. Number two was more alert, but still not sharp enough to save himself. Bolan detected him by following the rich aroma of tobacco smoke upwind, approaching from behind the gunner, moving stealthily. The blade in Bolan's hand was double-edged and razor-sharp.

He could have sworn, in retrospect, that there was nothing to alert the guard—no sound, however subtle; certainly no shadow to betray him in the midnight darkness—but the guy knew something, felt something. He had begun to turn, was reaching for his weapon when the blade passed underneath his jawline and released a crimson flood.

The dying sentry staggered backward, lost his footing and collapsed. One hand was pressed against his open throat, as if to dam the life escaping there; the other grazed his weapon, fluttered briefly there, and then withdrew.

How many left?

Bolan knew only one way to find out.

He finished skirting the perimeter, met no more sentries on the grounds and knew the rest of them had to be inside the villa, baby-sitting their employer. That there would be other guns, he had no doubt. It was ridiculous to think Tolya Valerik would be traveling with only two armed guards, both posted on first watch outside the house.

How many left? he asked himself again, already knowing it would make no difference what the answer was. Tolya

Valerik had been marked, and Bolan would proceed, regardless of the odds.

But he could use some luck.

His best approach would clearly be the patio, where French doors offered minimal defense against intruders. He could smash the glass there, shoot his way in if he had to, but the danger cut both ways. No lights were burning in the room that faced the patio, which told him any gunners lurking there had let their eyes adjust to darkness. They could scan the grounds, spot targets, open fire at will, while Bolan couldn't even say for sure if they were there.

He needed a diversion, something that would draw attention to the far side of the house. Two cars were parked out front, and it required only a moment for the Executioner to reach them, crouching in the shadowed space between a BMW and a Mercedes-Benz. The Beemer had a locking gas cap, but he caught a break with the Mercedes, no alarm sounds going off as Bolan opened up the little hatch, removed the cap and breathed in heady gas fumes.

Working in haste, he cut a thin strip from the bottom of his turtleneck and ripped it all the way around, inserting one end of the wick into the Merc's gas tank. He plugged the opening with gauze from his first-aid kit, took a lighter from his pocket, held it well below the line of sight from any window facing toward the cars, and thumbed it into glowing life. It took a moment for the fuse to catch, but then it flared and smoked, Bolan retreating in a crouch, watching the windows as he ran back toward the patio.

How long before the blast?

He had to estimate, since he had never timed a fuse cut from a cotton weave before. There was a chance it could burn out, he realized, but there had been no way for him to stay and watch the burn if the diversion were to serve its purpose.

He would simply have to wait.

The blast, when it came, was louder than Bolan expected, its shock wave rattling windows in the house, a smell of burning oil and rubber drifting to his nostrils on the breeze. The echo of the blast still rang in Bolan's ears when he heard worried voices raised inside the house, Valerik's soldiers rushing to defend their boss.

All moving toward the front, away from Bolan.

He rose and moved across the patio toward the French doors. If there were any shooters in the room beyond the glass, this was the time for them to open fire, while they could nail him in the open, well before he reached the house. When nothing happened, Bolan took for granted that his ruse had done its job.

The French doors would be locked, of course. He knew that, but he had to try them anyway, a quick shake to confirm his intuition. There was no way in without some noise, but he could do his best to keep it down, while the defenders of the house were concentrating on the blaze out front. The longer he delayed their recognition of a menace on their flank, the better Bolan's chance of taking them and coming out of the experience alive.

Instead of shooting out the lock, he swung an elbow, punched out one full pane of glass, and reached through with his left hand to release the latch. A heartbeat later, he was in, half crouching in the darkness of a sparsely furnished parlor, checking out the shadowed corners.

Nothing.

There were two ways out, besides the exit to the patio, and Bolan chose the one that seemed to lead in the direction where his enemies had gone, toward the front of the house. There was a light ahead of him, and muffled voices beckoning, although he couldn't understand a word they said.

He cleared the doorway, stepped into a hall that branched to left and right, as well as running arrow-straight ahead. He was about to join the party when a scuffling noise alerted him to movement on his right.

The shooter had apparently been sleeping, but the blast outside had roused him. Slower than the rest, he wore nothing but Jockey shorts and socks. Both hands were full, a Skorpion machine pistol clutched in his right, slacks dangling from his left.

At sight of Bolan, he released the pants and opened fire, full-auto, from a range of twenty feet.

THE MOMENT Suzanne made her move against the German shooter, Johnny knew they were in trouble—but he also knew they had a fighting chance. The gunners straight in front of him were momentarily distracted, helpless not to glance at Suzanne as she grappled with her captor, giving Johnny Gray a precious breather.

But he had to take care of the flankers, first.

It sounded like two guns on either side of him, all letting go at once, though Johnny had no time to stand around and count the muzzle-flashes. His opponents were experienced enough to place themselves so that their lines of fire didn't crisscross and take each other out.

Too bad, he thought, by which time he was facedown on the grass and angling to return fire with his Uzi. Left-hand gunners first, because his SMG was pointing that direction when he dropped, and now he had a fix on their positions, two men firing from the shrubbery, fifteen or twenty feet apart.

With bullets rippling overhead, he marked one muzzle-flash and hammered out a short burst, not waiting to determine its effect before he twisted, pivoting, and fired again. One of the shooters gave a high-pitched squeal of pain, and both ceased firing, though he knew that didn't guarantee a double kill.

No matter. He would take advantage of the moment while

it lasted, rolling over on his back, careful to keep his shoulders flat against the turf, instead of lurching up to meet the bullets that were still passing a foot or so above his face. The shooters had to have lost their fix on Johnny when he dropped, miscalculating his position in the darkness in their haste.

It was impossible to count rounds as the Uzi cranked them out, but he could estimate, milking the trigger for short. This time, he missed his first mark, had to try again, and by the time he got it right, Suzanne was crying out in pain somewhere behind him.

Dammit!

Johnny caught a break when the second gunner on his right got antsy, broke from cover in a rush, hoping to finish it at point-blank range, or maybe even hand-to-hand. It was a sucker move, despite the fact that he had found his range now, and his slugs were chewing up the grass a hand breadth from his target's face.

Instead of rolling clear and offering the man his unprotected back, Johnny held still and let the Uzi handle it, a stream of Parabellum shockers rising from the deck to meet the rifleman as he advanced. The slugs tore through his knees, thighs, stomach, chest, and slammed the smoking rifle from his grasp before he fell, a dazed expression on his lifeless face.

Suzanne was silent as he vaulted to his feet and moved to face the last of her tormentors. One of them was standing fast, sighting along the barrel of an AK-47, when the Uzi's last rounds sheared off his face in a crimson spray and punched him over backward into darkness.

Johnny let the Uzi drop, slapping against his hip, still dangling from its makeshift harness as he drew the CZ-75. The piece was double-action, no need to thumb the hammer back as he scanned for targets, spotting three in motion.

Three.

Was one of them Suzanne, or was she down below his line of fire? Without a light, the only way to tell for sure meant giving up his edge, letting his enemies fire first.

One of them seemed to read his mind, an automatic weapon stuttering, but he was hasty, nervous, and the burst missed Johnny by at least a yard. Before the shooter could correct his bearing, Johnny hit him with a double-tap and put him down, the last rounds from his SMG fanned skyward toward the stars.

Two figures still erect, and he was close enough to make out certain details now, a glint of errant moonlight on blond hair; the shiny, hairless skull behind Suzanne; the pistol wavering somewhere between primary targets, threatening them both.

"I must say, I'm impressed," the shooter said.

Ignoring him, Johnny addressed the prisoner. "Are you all right, Suzanne?"

"Shoot him!" she said. "For God's sake, do it!"

"Just relax," he cautioned her. "You know the way you tend to faint when you get too excited."

Suzanne understood immediately, stiffened in her captor's grasp—and then went limp, her head slumping forward, chin on chest. The bald guy tried to go with it, bending his knees, but the reaction was too little and too late. The double-tap from Johnny's pistol drilled him where his hairline should have been and dumped them both together on the grass.

TOLYA VALERIK heard the gunfire sputtering behind him, recognized that it was coming from inside the house and felt his blood run cold. The bastards had surrounded him, somehow. He was cut off, his limousine in flames outside. The tattered fragments of his life began to flash before his eyes.

"Tolya!" The gruff, familiar voice cut through his sudden blur of panic. Strong hands gripped his shoulders, shaking him as if he were a child. "Tolya! We have no time!"

He blinked at Anatoly Bogdashka, recognized his friend, the grim determination on his face. "No time," Valerik echoed, reading doom into the simple words.

"That's right!" Bogdashka snapped at him. "We have to go right now! The car—"

"The cars are burning, Anatoly! Don't you see?"

"The other car, for Christ's sake! In the barn, Tolya!"

The barn...

Of course. Valerik felt a sudden flush of shame at his debilitating panic. How could he forget something so basic to survival at the very moment when he needed it the most? It was humiliating, it was—

"Are you coming, damn it all?"

"I am."

He followed Bogdashka to the door, then hesitated as his chief lieutenant stepped into the firelight. There would certainly be gunmen waiting for them, sighting in to cut them down before they could proceed more than a few steps from the house. If he went out—

But Bogdashka wasn't falling. There were no shots from the darkness beyond the fiery hulks of the Mercedes and the BMW. In fact, Valerik realized, the only sounds of gunfire that he heard were those that echoed through the house itself. His people were returning fire, adding their thunder to the chorus, offering their lives in his defense.

A small force, like before, he thought. Three men, perhaps, or maybe two.

Valerik hesitated on the threshold, torn between a need to prove himself a man and desperate determination to survive at any cost to dignity. If he was seen to run again...

Bogdashka grabbed him by the collar of his jacket, fairly dragged him into the firelight, tugging him across the porch and down the wooden steps into the yard. Valerik did not fight him, told himself it was the acrid pall of smoke that brought tears to his eyes. There was no shame in living to retaliate against your enemies another day.

The sounds of combat from inside the house intensified, as Bogdashka tugged and hurried him across the yard in the direction of the barn. If he was forced to bet, Valerik would have wagered that the men he'd left behind would never tell his story to another living soul.

They wouldn't have the chance.

"He's killing them!" Valerik blurted out, not certain in his mind who he was, terrified that if he lingered, he might learn the answer to that final question with his dying breath.

"Better them than us," Bogdashka said. "Come on, goddammit!"

There was no lock on the barn, although the door was closed. Valerik had supposed the lock to be superfluous while he had sentries posted in the yard. Where were they? he wondered, knowing with a certainty the guards were dead. How else could anyone have torched the cars and made his way inside the house?

Bogdashka dragged one of the wooden doors back, scraping dirt along the way. "Tolya! The other one!" he barked, Valerik moving like a zombie to the second door, putting his weight behind it as it grudgingly began to yield.

Their backup vehicles were parked inside the old converted barn. There was a Porsche and a Range Rover, one for speed, the other chosen for its rugged durability. Without a word of consultation, taking charge, Bogdashka climbed behind the Rover's steering wheel and fired up the engine. Valerik had to hurry, circling to climb in on the other side, afraid that Bogdashka might drive off and leave him there.

Across the firelit yard, Valerik saw a tall man dressed in black emerging from the front door of his villa, some kind of automatic rifle in his hands. Before he had a chance to speak, warn Bogdashka, they were moving, wheeling hard left in a U-turn that would put the barn between them and the house if only they had time.

A bullet drilled the Range Rover's back window, sizzled past Valerik's face and clipped the rearview mirror as it took out a fist-sized portion of the windshield out.

"Fuck you!" Bogdashka cackled like a madman, pounding on the steering wheel. "We made it, fuck your mother! We're alive!"

But for how long? Valerik wondered.

DECKARD HAD them now.

There was Vassily Krestyanov, together with the giant who chauffeured him around, and two more soldiers who could only be a part of the security detachment. Not that they would do Krestyanov any good the way they were, all loaded down with baggage.

It was perfect.

Deckard had reloaded on his way upstairs, determined not to face his adversaries with a partly empty magazine. The Ingram burned up ammunition fast enough without him giving up a vital edge.

But now he had the bastards where he wanted them, Krestyanov turning toward him only now, too late, Deckard enjoying the expression on the Russian's face.

"I'm glad you're packed," he said, unable to resist the quip, "because it's checkout time."

Krestyanov had a briefcase in his left hand, nothing in his right. The giant was empty-handed, which seemed odd to Deckard, even more so with the way he stood, broad shoulders hunched, his right arm crooked, held close against his side, like he was carrying a football down the field...or maybe something else.

Deckard was focused on the giant when Krestyanov made his move. Instead of reaching for a gun, the colonel grabbed the nearest body he could reach and dragged the startled man in front of him, using the luggage bearer as a human shield. While Krestyanov was doing that, the giant whipped some kind of compact automatic weapon out from underneath his coat, firing one-handed, without even taking time to aim.

It was a textbook case of how a perfect set could go to hell.

Recoiling from the muzzle-flare of what appeared to be a short Kalashnikov, Deckard depressed the Ingram's trigger, blazing off the whole damned magazine within a second and a half. He saw the man in front of Krestyanov begin to shimmy, taking hits, but Deckard's hollowpoint rounds weren't about to penetrate and give him two-for-one. The impact staggered Krestyanov, but he maintained his grip on the cadaver, dragging it along with him as Deckard heard the elevator chime and saw the door slide open.

Shit!

He ducked and stumbled backward toward the doorway and the service stairs, the only cover handy, while the giant blazed away with his Kalashnikov. Deckard retrieved another mag and ditched the empty, felt the bullets cutting through his trench coat, furrowing his side, oblivious to pain.

Both of the luggage handlers were down, he saw that now, a victory of sorts, though one of them still moved, groping inside his tattered, bloody jacket for a weapon. Deckard left him to it, aiming for the giant as he burned up half the second magazine, watching great clouds of plaster dust explode from mutilated walls.

The hulk was too damned fast, despite his size, long-legging toward the elevator, ducking as he slipped inside, a parting burst from the AK that came close enough to ruffle Deckard's hair.

And they were gone, the elevator door shut, his bullets thunking ineffectually into solid steel. The wounded soldier, on all fours, reached out to grab his leg, and Deckard used the Glock to finish him, a clean shot through the scalp, before he turned and sprinted for the stairs.

It was too late, he knew, but still he had to try. If he could just get one more shot at Krestyanov, put one round out of thirty-two inside the bull's-eye, he could still redeem this hideous snafu.

He took the service stairs in leaps and bounds, risking a broken leg or worse with every step, bruising himself against the walls each time he reached another landing. Before he made it halfway to the lobby level, Deckard's ears were ringing, and he felt as if he had been beaten with a baseball bat from head to knees.

He stumbled on the next-to-last flight down, pitched forward, surfing facedown to the landing where he huddled, semiconscious, vaguely thankful that the Ingram hadn't gone off in his face as he was plunging down the stairs. He struggled to his feet, all sense of time deserting him, and staggered down the last flight to the ground floor, sagged into the lobby with a smell of gunsmoke lingering, the open elevator mocking him.

Too goddamned late.

The clerk was staring at him, dumbstruck. Deckard pondered the idea of shooting him, then shrugged it off and hobbled past him toward the street.

"I CAN'T BELIEVE I missed them both, for Christ's sake." Able Deckard shook his head again, his eyes closed, his features molded in a scowl. "And Keane...I never even saw him. Shit!"

"We all missed," Bolan said, "except for Johnny."

Sitting on the hotel bed with Johnny close beside her, Suzanne King looked none the worse for wear. A few small bruises and abrasions, but compared to Deckard—black and blue, as if he had been soundly beaten, and swathed in gauze and tape to seal a bullet graze on his left side—the woman came off looking fresh enough to win a beauty pageant.

"I got lucky," Johnny said, "and Suzanne helped a lot. I didn't recognize the shooters, though, in what time I had to check them out. None of the heavies in attendance, definitely."

Deckard cleared his throat. "You said a bald guy led the snatch team?"

Johnny and Suzanne nodded together. "Not just bald," Suzanne elaborated. "He was completely hairless."

Now it was Deckard's turn to nod. "Okay, I know him, then. Same guy I spotted at the beer garden with Krestyanov and his pet circus freak. It took a while to run the descriptions through Langley, but I finally heard back."

"So, share," Johnny said.

"Manfred Berghoff. Former Stasi, which would explain his line to Krestyanov. The KGB was Stasi's very own Big Brother program."

"What about the big man?" Bolan asked.

"The one I missed, you mean," Deckard said bitterly. "Name's Nikolai Lukasha. Word is that he worked with Krestyanov before Vassily left the KGB, and when his buddy walked, Lukasha tagged along. He wasn't any good for undercover work, big as he is, but he enjoyed the wet work when a job came up that didn't call for total anonymity. Also, he spent a lot of time around the Lubyanka, handling interrogations. Guy's a prince, and I just let him waltz away."

"You'll have another chance to make it good," Bolan replied, "unless you're giving up."

"You kidding me?" Deckard was working on a smile, not quite achieving it. "Just tell me where and when. I'm there."

"Well, that's the problem," Bolan said. "I kind of hoped that you could tell us when and where. We're not exactly in the loop right now, you get my drift."

Deckard was nodding, seemed about to answer, when

Johnny cleared his throat almost theatrically. "Before we lay another road trip on," he said, "we need to think about Suzanne."

"Hey, guys," she told the room at large, "I'm fine. Okay, I didn't count on getting kidnapped, but it all worked out, right?"

"Depends on how you look at it," Bolan stated. "It's a good thing that you're safe and sound, of course. It would have been a better thing if there had been no kidnapping to start with."

"Well, of course, but—"

"What I'm saying is, if one of us had had an extra gun last night—" his nod included Deckard "—then at least a portion of our problem might be solved right now."

"Now, wait a second—" Johnny's face had clouded over, darkening with anger.

"No," Suzanne's clear voice cut through his protest. "No, he's absolutely right. This whole damned thing's my fault. Again. You wouldn't even be here, if I hadn't kept on looking for my brother."

"That isn't what I meant," Bolan said, cutting off the flow of Suzanne's guilt. "I'm glad we're here. If we had missed this thing—whatever it turns out to be—I have a feeling we'd regret it, big time. At this moment, though, we need complete and undiluted focus on the mission. No sideshows."

"I understand," she said. "Just tell me what to do."

"I'd like to fix you up with travel papers, find some neutral ground and stash you there until this thing is finished, one way or another."

"Switzerland?" Johnny asked.

Bolan shrugged. "It's close," he said. "Why not? If you have cash—and we've got plenty—I suspect the Swiss won't ask too many questions."

"Hey, I'm there," the lady said. "Just point me toward the airplane."

Bolan felt as if a weight had vanished from his shoulders, and despite the grim expression on his brother's face, he knew Johnny had to feel the same relief, deep down. "Okay, then," he continued, "all we have to do, now, is locate our targets."

"It shouldn't be that big a problem," Deckard said.

"How's that?" Bolan asked skeptically.

"I mean, if I got my ass kicked repeatedly, as bad as Tolya and Vassily have, there's only one place I'd feel safe."

"Which is?"

"I'd head for home," Deckard said.

"Russia." When Johnny spoke the word, it came out sounding flat and dead.

"That would be my guess," Deckard said. "Who's up for borscht?"

* * * * *

Don't miss the exciting conclusion of
THE CONSPIRACY TRILOGY
Look for JUDGMENT DAY
on sale May 2001.

James Axler

OUTLANDERS®

PURGATORY ROAD

The fate of humanity remains ever uncertain, dictated by the obscure forces that have commandeered mankind's destiny for thousands of years. The plenipotentiaries of these ancient oppressors—the nine barons who have controlled America in the two hundred years since the nukecaust—are now falling prey to their own rabid desire for power.

Book #3 of *The Imperator Wars* saga, a trilogy chronicling the introduction of a new child imperator—launching the baronies into war!

**Gold Eagle brings you
high-tech action and mystic adventure!**

THE

Destroyer™

#123 DISLOYAL OPPOSITION

Created by
MURPHY
and SAPIR

THE RUSTED CURTAIN BOOK 1

A secret Russian particle-beam weapon has long been suspected as responsible for the space shuttle Challenger explosion. Many scoffed…until the old Soviet Union dissolves and the weapon is sold on the Russian black market to the ruling council of Barkley, California—the most famous enclave of unrepentant socialists in the Western World. They direct it at American skies, making no planes, satellites or space shuttles safe until their very heavy price is paid.

Available in April 2001 at your favorite retail outlet.